Father F'in' Christmas

A Minded Story

Father F'in' Christmas

A Minded Story

By

R.L. Merrill

Dedication

To my grandmother, Constance Greene. Thank you for bringing the bright spot to my Christmases since 1974. I love you.

Chapter One

"Tommy, you've been here for some time. It's time for you to share your story."

Just like being caught dozing in history class, I jerked in my chair and sucked in a breath through my nose.

Funny, the last thing I remember was a goddamned fireball knocking me backwards off the ladder. Why don't I smell no smoke?

"Tommy?"

Why the fuck is some old lady with her knitting staring at me? And why am I back in the school gym?

"I think Thomas here is having a rather unpleasant flashback. Too much LSD, mate? Thought they tested you blokes for drugs in the good old FDNY."

I looked to my left and this fucking guy with a Mohawk had a smirk on his mug that made me want to slap the shit out of him.

If I could move.

"It's alright, dear. Sometimes it takes our group members a long time before they become aware. You've taken the first step by joining us, so welcome."

I really wish she'd quit smiling at me like I was a poor fool to be pitied. I knew I'd gotten myself into this mess. But I wasn't about to go all twelve-step here. Sure, I was drinkin' on the job, but that's not why I fell.

"It sure didn't help," Mohawk Guy said. The idiot even had safety pins through his ears and along the seam of his vest like some punk rock reject from the '70s or '80s.

"What the fuck's your problem, Pin Cushion? You keep running your mouth and I'll—"

"You'll what? Bloody hell, I hate dealing with D.D.S. You're dead, mate. Get on with it."

"Who pissed in your Wheaties? I know I'm fucking dead, alright? Now what's this D.D.S?" I reached for the flask in my boot, knowing the feel of the cool metal in my hand would make this shit go away. But my arm wouldn't do what I told it to.

"Why can't I move? Oh, shit! I'm paralyzed, ain't I? From when I fell."

"You no longer have your physical body, Tommy. The reason you can't move is that you are in denial. Death Denial Syndrome, to be exact. Your soul has not yet accepted its demise. You're here with us, in this group, to help you accept your mortality and decide how you would like to spend your afterlife."

For the first time, I noticed a few other people sitting around the circle of folding chairs. Some guy wearing a baker's uniform, a couple of soldiers, a mechanic in coveralls... The smell of sweaty socks hit me straight on, making my eyes water. I rubbed at them to stop the assault.

I rubbed at my face.

"There you are. How does that feel?"

"I'm movin'," I whispered, looking down at my hands. The scars from that three-alarm we put out two years ago were still there. I'd had to slip off my heavy gloves to get my fingers to work, unlatching the dog crate where a little girl had climbed inside with her puppy to hide. She'd slammed the door shut and it somehow latched itself. Nearly lost the both of them. That was before the first accident.

"Great. I wiggled my fingers. Can I go now?"

"And where would you like to go?"

I stared blankly at her. *That's right. I'm dead.* A thought slammed into my head so hard, I winced.

Kimberly.

"Yeah, that's right. You're dead and your lovely wife remained behind to pick up the pieces. Boo fucking hoo," Mohawk muttered.

I shot to my feet. "You want to go, ya limey piece of shit? I'll rip those pins outta your ears and shove them right up your ass, you fucking—"

"Sit down, Tommy."

For some reason, my body obeyed the old woman when my mind wanted to lash out at this fucking guy.

She stared me down over the rim of her glasses, her hands paused in whatever she was knitting. I eased back into the chair and my body relaxed, waiting for her to go on.

"Louis?"

Mohawk Guy gave her a sneer that would have gotten his hands whacked with a ruler back at St. Luke's.

"Oh, come on!" he shouted at her. "You can't expect—"

"I can and I do. You will mind your manners and allow Tommy the chance to become aware and make his choice. Sometimes I think you could truly use a woman's touch in your work."

Mohawk Guy obviously didn't like being dressed down in front of the group. Served him right, the bastard.

"Now Tommy, the practice is that our members share their stories with the group in order to help them determine how to move on from here. This is merely a temporary layover, so do not fret."

"What about my wife?" The words choked me, like being on scene without my mask.

"That is a situation I think we may want to discuss. But first. Your story, please. You won't be able to move on—"

"Right, right. Unburden yourself and then go on to the fucking Elysian Fields or some shit."

"Not exactly, but yes. You do carry a burden. Please, tell us."

I felt compelled to speak, as though my body was once again following the rules of the old woman rather than my simple command to shut the hell up.

"I had an accident not too long ago. A year. We responded to an apartment fire, no big deal. Hadn't spread, no other units were threatened. Fire was mostly contained. So I'm checking the perimeter and I see this fucking cat. It's trapped up on a ledge on the third floor, too afraid to move. I couldn't figure out how it got there, and all I kept hearing was my Kimberly—"

Pain lanced my chest at the sound of her name falling from my lips. I could be a tough guy all I wanted, but her name fucking slayed me.

"All I kept thinking was that my wife would be pissed if she knew I didn't try to save this fucking cat. So I got up on the ladder and was just about to the spot I'd seen it, when the damn thing leaped past me and scrambled onto a fucking tree limb next to the building. I reached toward it, trying to call the damn thing closer, and my foot slipped. I tried to grab the ladder but missed and ended up hanging from the ledge until my guys could get the ladder moved back under me. Scariest minute or so of my life. All I could think of was who would take care of my Kimberly? Who would make sure she ate, wore a coat when it was cold? We both knew I had a dangerous job, but I felt pretty damn invincible up 'til that point. When I got down, I got fucking drunk as a skunk…and after that? I was no good. Ruined. A fuckin' fireman who's afraid a' heights."

Then booze. And more booze and more booze.

"Helped you forget, didn't it? And then you were fucked."

One of the soldiers nodded. I hadn't seen him speak, but he obviously felt my pain.

"Yeah," was all I said. We maintained eye contact for what felt like an hour. And for all I know it coulda been. I wondered what his story was, whether all of these people here had fucked up like I had.

"So then what happened?"

A woman I hadn't noticed before across the room spoke up. She wore a bus driver's uniform. She'd probably seen some shit.

"I don't know. I kept going to work, I got reassigned off the ladder, told the chief I didn't feel right. He said he'd give me a few months, sent me to the shrink. I bullshitted my way through therapy, and then I kept old faithful close to me at all times."

I reached down and nearly sighed out loud at how good the metal felt in my hand. I pulled it out and unscrewed the cap, tipping my head and—

"You didn't seriously think you could drink that in here, did you? You're quite daft."

"Shut the fuck up, asshole."

The soldier didn't seem too happy with Mohawk Guy either. It was nice to know I wasn't the only one he was bothering.

"Anyway, I guess I kept it *too* close because on my last job, I was pretty fucked up. I'd been put back on the ladder, the chief had no one else, you know? Anyway, fucking gas explosion knocks me back and here I am."

Pretty pathetic, I should have added. I wouldn't have been able to handle it if any of these clowns started saying I was a fucking hero. I was never that guy, no matter what Kimberly may have thought. She was the fucking hero. *My hero.*

"Being drunk on the job put your crew in danger. That was selfish, dawg," the quiet soldier said.

The one who'd spoken up before elbowed him and muttered something.

"Don't you think I know that? I didn't have a choice."

"You could have requested a leave," the bus driver said.

"Who the fuck are you people to tell me what to do? I know I fucked up! I'm dead, aren't I? It's not like I killed anyone else."

"Actually," the old woman said slowly, her eyes focused on her knitting now. "When you fell, you caused the serious injury of one of your crew, and another died in the blast. It was a terrible day for the New York Fire Department. You were not found to be at fault, however."

I caused this. It was my fault, I don't care what anyone says. This is on me.

"You did a lot of stupid shite, mate, but this one isn't on you. Of course, if you hadn't been hammered—"

I stood and kicked back my chair...for what? I was dead. What the fuck was I going to do? I turned and faced the blackness surrounding our circle in the middle of the gymnasium floor. I could barely see two feet in front of my face. There were no other sounds, only the fidgeting of the people in the circle. Is that what death would have in store for me? Pitch blackness? Suffocating silence?

A gentle hand rested between my shoulder blades and I flinched away. No one should get their hands dirty on my account. My chest rose and fell like I was breathing, but no air passed through my lips.

"You have suffered, Tommy. You have sacrificed. You made some poor choices, and sadly you perished because of one of them. Whether the report said that or not, you know it's true, don't you?"

"You don't hold nothing back, do ya?" My cheeks were wet all of a sudden. *The fuck? I don't fucking cry.*

"What if I told you that you could make some of it right? Make a difference?"

That stabbing sensation where my heart should've been hurt more than any burn I'd ever had, more than breaking my collarbone during high school football or even fracturing my pelvis on the hose during fire academy. I'd never felt anything like it, hollow, dull, persistent, everlasting...

"You can give your wife closure. You can make amends to your crew. You can choose to intervene, and then you must choose your existence."

"My existence? You mean like heaven or hell?"

"It's not as clear cut as that," she said softly behind me.

I still couldn't face her. "I can see Kimberly?"

The old woman paused before answering. "You can make a difference in her life. Only *you* know what that difference should be. You will have the power to manipulate her circumstances for the better, give her the gift of a better life."

"What, like Santa Claus, giving gifts and shit?"

"No, he has his hands full giving gifts to young children. However, we do need assistants to represent Father Christmas, doing good deeds, granting wishes... That is actually an option you might consider for your afterlife."

"Right. Father Fuckin' Christmas. I'm your poster boy. You're crazy, lady, if you think I—"

"You will have help. I am sending our best Intervention Specialist with you. He's been performing these tasks for—"

"Too bloody long."

I spun around, and there stood fucking Mohawk Guy, lighting a cigarette.

"You're kidding, right? This fucking guy?"

The old woman sighed and returned to her seat, picking up her knitting. It hadn't grown in length since we'd been sitting here. I'd watched, wondering what the fuck she was making with her blue yarn. Looking around, I saw that the three of us were now alone in the circle.

"The others have their own denials to overcome and they will have similar opportunities to mind their kin. It is time for you and Louis to depart. Are you ready?"

"Wait! How will I know what to do? What—"

"You can trust Louis. He's our best."

I looked over this "specialist": tall and pale, torn denim with jackboots, leather jacket, black hair standing about seven inches off his scalp. And that superior-looking set to his mouth. I wanted to smash him in the face with a fucking folding chair. What the fuck was this guy going to tell me about what *my* woman needed?

"You are truly a piece of work. Look, we'll see to her future, set events in motion to provide her with some happiness, blah blah blah, and then you'll be on your way to either a new existence, or you can blink out. Makes no difference to me."

"You're like some kind of mind reader? Look, stay the fuck outta my head. You don't know me, you British fucktard."

Mohawk guy rolled his eyes. "Are you *quite* finished? Can we be on our way now?"

Somehow we were now alone and outside the gym doors.

"What the...? How the hell?"

"Let me attempt to explain this to you with your limited mental capacity. There are rules. You follow them. You do what I say. You may not leave my presence or you will end up right back in group. Argue with my instructions or put one boot out of line and I will send your arse right back here. When your time is up, no matter the outcome—"

"I know, I know. My ass will be sent right back here. Got it. But you're going to help me make things right for Kimberly, for real? She don't deserve to suffer for what I've done."

"Sparky, I don't give a damn about you, or anyone else for that matter. I have a job to do, whether I like it or not, and I do what I'm told. End of story."

Sparky? "So now you're a funny guy, huh?"

"I'm a laugh a minute. Come on, let's go see to your wife."

Chapter Two

"Come and ride my sleigh, baby!"

"I got yer jingle balls right here!"

"Show us your tits!"

For as long as I have been conscious, I've watched over the city of San Francisco. I've witnessed many Christmas seasons and it never ceases to amaze me how awful people can be to each other. Take for example this party going on in the penthouse across from my building. A bunch of drunken guys dressed like elves were loudly cheering on a stripper in a sexy Santa outfit. She was not the most graceful dancer I'd ever seen, but she had big tits, and that seemed to make the guys all the more excited.

I'd never quite understood what it was about tits that turned men into slobbering maniacs, but I'd seen many men in that penthouse stick their faces in the middle of a big pair, shake their heads violently, and come away happy. The men up there had wild parties frequently, but the only women in attendance seemed to be hired help.

It takes all kinds, I suppose.

Santa's Little Stripper did her thing and tried to leave graciously, but the men were pawing all over her until she finally broke away and ran out the door, a look of fear on her face. I wondered why she'd chosen, or if she'd chosen, to do this kind of thing. I'd seen several examples of women doing things they didn't necessarily want to do in that penthouse.

So yeah, I'm a gargoyle, and I watch over the city. I'm not sure how I came to be here or what my purpose is other than to observe. I can see and hear, but that's about it. The building across from mine had many viewing opportunities, but I had my favorites. The redhead on the 36th floor gave me impure thoughts. The businessman right below her had a carousel of male lovers in and out of his apartment. And the sweet lady who lived next door to the redhead had great taste in movies and a whole bunch of cats. She intrigued me because, unlike the other tenants, she was home most of the time and she never had another person inside. She watched movies, played with her cats, and cried a lot. I often wondered why she was so sad. She definitely seemed lonely.

I could relate to lonely. For so long, I've watched others living their lives and wanted to be a part of what they usually took for granted. I had so many questions. Just because I'm a rock doesn't mean I have no feelings. I feel very deeply.

A ruckus erupted in the penthouse, drawing me from my thoughts. Elves punched elves. Beer bottles and chairs went flying. A Christmas tree was thrown through the window onto the balcony. There was blood. There was puke. A security guard busted in the door, took one look at the mess and called for backup.

Yeah. Christmas. What a jolly holiday.

Chapter Three

Pin Cushion and I walked and walked until the sky began to lighten around us. A foggy street at dawn? Kinda reminded me of New York City on those mornings I'd be out washing the rig in the bitter cold, my breath visible around me. But these buildings were all wrong for New York. I realized the asshole was talking so I figured I should pay attention.

"San Francisco. Seems your old lady wanted to get as far away from her past as possible. She's been here, what, about four years now? She tried to make things work—"

"Hold up. Did you just say four fucking years? What year is this?"

Mohawk guy, or Louis, whatever the fuck his name was, finally stopped walking. He cursed under his breath and lit another cigarette.

"Hey how come you can smoke those things but I can't drink?"

Louis blew out a puff of smoke and dropped his head back on his shoulders. "I said you couldn't drink back there. In group. Things are different out here."

"So I can drink? Hell yeah! Show me to the nearest liquor store."

Louis turned on me and got all up in my face, which was pretty brave for a scrawny piece of shit like him. He mighta had a couple inches on me, but I outweighed him by at least fifty pounds.

"Only because you drank yourself stupid and quit caring about your body, you ignorant prick. Some of us didn't have the luxury of eating for five every day. And no drink for you, not until we're through."

This fucking guy. "Whatever. You didn't answer me. What year is it?"

His expression changed from pissed to just plain sad. "Time moves differently in the afterlife. You'll find that out soon enough. You died five years ago, mate."

Five years. She's been alone for five years. Wait…

"She's still alone. And quite broken up over your demise, surprisingly."

"Hey, you watch yourself. I used to be quite a looker before shit—"

"Right. Anyhoo, she lives in this building with several hairy beasts. Lucky for her, you had a sweet life insurance plan so she could afford to live here. She'll be leaving for work…now."

I followed his line of sight to see a woman leaving the building and walking away from us. Without thinking, my feet followed, but this didn't seem like my Kimberly. This woman, from what I could see of her through her bulky clothes, looked too thin. She also didn't have Kimberly's telltale meander. I used to tease her all the time because when we'd walk together, she'd run into me constantly. She walked like a fucking drunk, never in a straight line, and rarely with any sense of what was around her. What's worse was that half the time, she'd have her nose in a book and wouldn't be paying attention, even walking down the street back home in Jersey. She got clipped by a cab once, broke her damn leg. I'll never forget the panic I felt when my chief told me and rushed me to the ER to meet her...

"Wait up," Louis called out to me. His long legs ate up the space between us in three strides.

"You sure that's her? She don't look right."

"Being a grieving widow will do that to a woman," he said.

I turned on him, my hands balled into fists. "You this much of an asshole all the time? Because I'm getting sick of your fucking mouth."

Louis shrugged. "Pretty much. You'd better get used to it, as we're stuck together until you figure out how to fix this mess."

Up ahead of us, Kimberly caught a trolley and we hurried to hop on before it pulled too far from the stop. It fucking hurt knowing she couldn't see me, that I couldn't just go up and approach her. Sure enough, she pulled out a book, one of her mysteries. My lip twitched up in a smile as I counted how many times she pushed her glasses up her nose. Five...six...seven...

Soon the trolley stopped and she got off. A few more blocks of walking and we watched as she entered the San Francisco Animal Care and Control building. Louis gestured for us to follow her inside. It was weird that we just walked right in and nobody seemed to notice the door opening and closing by itself.

"People see and hear what they want. No one will notice us unless it's time."

"Right. Like ghosts and shit."

"Whatever."

Kimberly went behind a counter and took off her heavy wool coat. I recognized it as the one I got her for our first Christmas being married. She'd acted like she was in love with it, but then her mom let me know she was allergic to wool. She'd still worn it, said it didn't really touch her skin or anything. Was I such an asshole that I didn't notice she scratched at her neck when she took it off, like she was doing right now?

"Yeah, you really were."

"Shut up! How the hell are you doing that anyway?"

Louis rolled his eyes. "Some people broadcast more than others. You're an open book. It's quite an annoying character flaw you have there."

Kimberly'd left the office area and was climbing a set of stairs, so I followed her, or else I would have chewed old Pin Cushion out.

We spent the whole day watching her take out the cats and play with them, checking their charts, feeding them and cleaning up their litter. Even the most skittish ones came right up to her. She'd always had a magic touch with animals. I'd only allowed her to have one cat, Johnson, when we were married. I couldn't stand the damn things, but I hated to say no.

She only smiled when she talked to the cats. Her co-workers were all very nice to her, but I watched them as they walked away, giving her that look I'd always hated. She was awkward, sure. She never quite fit in anywhere, but from the moment I'd lain eyes on her at school when she'd transferred in our senior year, I knew I had to have her. She was so quirky and adorable, she'd had no idea how beautiful she was.

And she'd hated me.

No one hated me. I made it my mission to make her fall in love with me because I knew she'd make a good wife, wouldn't ever cheat or be a pain in the ass about shopping and spending too much fucking money. And frankly, I was tired of banging cheerleaders and party girls. Turned out, once we got married? She was insatiable. I never went without. Until I became a drunk, that is.

I realized on the ride back to her apartment that Kimberly had never eaten lunch. I used to have to remind her sometimes to eat because she'd get so involved in whatever she was doing. With no one to remind her, she was wasting the fuck away. Her face had once been round and bright, with rosy patches on her cheeks. Now? She was pale and bony, her eyes surrounded by darkness.

"She's not well, your widow. We are intervening now, before…"

"Before what? What the fuck aren't you telling me?" I'd wanted to punch this fucking guy a million times already, but this time I was ready to throttle his scrawny ass.

He seemed to be working up to something, but I was distracted by her movements in the kitchen. I turned him around so he wouldn't watch as she stripped out of her work uniform and threw her clothes into a stackable washing machine. My heart broke at seeing her too-thin body. She hadn't just lost weight. She was seriously wasting away.

"It's true what they say, that people can die from a broken heart."

His words slammed into me like that damn gas explosion.

Broken heart.

My fault.

My responsibility to fix it.

I heard the shower running, so I took a more thorough look around. I recognized some of the knickknacks from our place, her damn cat figurines and framed pictures of us throughout the years we'd been married. We'd just celebrated our tenth wedding anniversary when I had my first fuckup. A year later, I was dead. That was five years ago.

Louis lit up another cigarette as we stood in her living room. She returned from her shower wrapped in a fluffy pink bathrobe and went from cat to cat, saying hello and giving them cuddles or a scratch behind the ears. They were all acting a little rambunctious, like something had them upset. She eventually settled on the couch and pulled something out from behind a pillow.

My FDNY sweatshirt.

She held it to her face and inhaled. Then the damn waterworks started.

I wanted to comfort her, wanted to reveal myself or some shit.

Instead, Louis somehow flashed us outside, back on the street.

"What the fuck?! We can't just leave her like that!"

"Aren't you a genius. What do you suppose we do?"

"What *can* we do? It's not like I can come back to life and we can pick back up, and she sure as hell ain't gonna just take up with some other fucking guy."

Louis laughed. "Ego much? You really think you were that fantastic in the sack she won't ever take another lover?"

"Well, I ain't saying that. I just know Kimberly. She took our vows to heart, you know? She won't just sleep around, she'd never do that. The only way she'd ever be with someone else is if…"

I had a plan.

Chapter Four

The next morning, I followed behind Louis as he entered the Animal Care center. Kimberly was working the front desk and gave him a curious look.

"Can I help you?" she asked, trying not to stare at the safety pins in his ears and failing miserably.

Louis, God bless him, looked horribly uncomfortable.

"I suppose." He looked around with a frown and I kicked him in the leg.

"*Bollocks*," he whispered sharply, giving me an ugly look.

"I'm sorry? Are you alright?"

Being this close to Kimberly was difficult. I missed her. We didn't have the best marriage ever, but she was the best friend I ever had. I don't think I ever told her that.

"I'm fine. I guess I'd like to see your collection of pu— Cats. Your cats. For adoption."

I'd smacked him in the head when he almost slipped and said that word. What a moron. "You can't talk to her like that," I said to him up close to his ear.

He shot me a look over his shoulder and turned back hurriedly so she wouldn't catch him.

"Well," she said, looking at him like he was a freak. "You can see what we have, but there's an application process. You can't just walk in and get a cat, you know."

She turned around and grabbed a key from the board behind her. When she turned back, she stared once again.

"Doesn't that hurt? Sticking those in your ears? I knew a guy back in Jersey who tried it once. Passed out on my cousin Sheila's bathroom floor. I got my ears pierced at the mall with Sandy and that hurt like hell. I can only imagine—"

"Right. The cats?"

I kicked him again and he lurched forward, nearly running into her. This was kind of fun, getting him back for all the asshole things he'd said to me.

"Do you live in an apartment? Are you in the city? Because if you rent, your landlord has to approve."

"I'm between places right now," he answered with a smirk. When she frowned, he tried to cover it by saying, "The cat is actually for my gran. She wants one. I thought it would be a nice surprise."

They were now upstairs and entering the room where they kept cages for the little hairy beasts. She continued talking to him in that rambling way she always did and I could see he was getting flustered. As the door closed, he stepped closer to her.

"Now, this guy is a bit older, but older cats can make great companions because it's like they just know, you know, that you are giving them a second chance and—"

As she opened the cage door, the cat backed into a corner and started hissing as if the devil himself were standing there. I remembered hearing something about cats freaking out around the dead or some shit. This oughta be interesting.

"Huh, that's strange. He's never acted like that before."

A large black cat in the cage directly behind Louis began growling, causing the guy to jump. He turned around and backed up, getting dangerously close to another cage. Before he could get away, the black cat inside swiped at his ear through the bars and hooked one of his safety pins.

"Bloody hell!" he screeched as the cat tugged. Kimberly hurried over and tried to untangle the two of them, but her hands came away covered in Louis's blood.

"Are these creatures all insane? They're a deadly menace, the whole lot of 'em!"

Kimberly apologized profusely and closed the cage door she'd been opening.

"Let me get you cleaned up in here," she said, pushing him not so gently to a counter with a first-aid kit on it. "Cat scratches can cause infection and can make you very ill."

Louis calmed down and his expression softened. He looked her over curiously as she prepared gauze with some antiseptic cleanser.

"I suppose I'm not meant to be a cat owner."

She shook her head as she began cleaning his wound. "They're not for everyone. My ex-husband hated them. He let me have one, but he bitched about it all the time. You know that cat hated him right back? Anyway, maybe you're more of a dog person."

"I don't know," Louis said, and fuck me, but his lip curled up in a smile that was dangerously flirtatious. "Perhaps I just need the right woman."

She kept cleaning him up, not missing a beat. "Cats are better than people. They don't talk back or disappoint you. Feed them and take care of them and they're loyal forever."

"Don't you think a person could be loyal forever? At least a person can carry on a conversation…"

"I talk to my cats all the time. They're all the entertainment I need."

Louis turned his body and crowded her against the counter a bit. If she noticed, she didn't seem to mind. She disposed of the gauze and spread some cream on a clean piece. She turned to put it on his ear, but instead she froze. Her eyes widened in surprise at his proximity.

"Don't you miss having a man around?"

"I do miss sex," she blurted out, then blinked her eyes shut and shook her head. "God, I'm such a clod. My ex-husband used to tell me all the time that I needed a filter, that I just said whatever I thought."

"Nothing wrong with that, love." He moved even closer, taking her hands in his. "Would you like to find love again?"

Something changed on her expression, like she was in a trance or something. "I...I can't. My husband..."

"Is dead," Louis said softly.

A tear ran down her cheek. "It doesn't feel right to think about being with someone else. It's like I'm cheating."

"What if I said you could have great sex again with the man of your dreams?"

She blinked once. "No way The Rock is gonna show up on my doorstep, so that's out of the question." She snorted a laugh and Louis actually smiled.

Jesus. She still has the hots for that fucking guy.

"But what if he did? Would you open your door for him?"

"Who are you?"

"I'm here to bring you a Christmas Wish. Now, would you open your door?"

Kimberly nodded slowly. "I would let him in."

Watching him hypnotize Kimberly, or whatever the fuck he was doing, was so fascinating, I forgot to be pissed about him being all up in her space.

"That's good, that's really good. He's going to knock on your door tonight and you're going to let him in, despite the fact he'll say he's not Dwayne Johnson. He'll be yours for a night to do with whatever you wish. Will you let him make love to you?"

She nodded in that dazed way again.

I had to leave the room. I'd had enough. Mentally, I knew she and I were through, that there was no way I could ever touch her again. That didn't make me any less pissed off about this scenario. But in my heart, I knew this was the right thing to do. She'd put up with my shit over the years, especially that last year when I was drunk all the time. I never once laid a hand on her, but I was a bastard. I figured I'd ruined everything and she'd leave me. But she didn't. Faithful to the bitter fucking end. Well, if I was going to do right by her, she at least deserved some happiness, even if it was for a short time.

Through the door, I saw Louis say a few more things to her and then he disappeared. She jerked forward in his absence, her hand flying to her chest in shock. It took her several moments to compose herself.

Louis appeared at my side, and the last thing I saw before he yanked me away was her smile.

Outside her building on the sidewalk, it was time to devise the next part of the plan.

"So how do we get The Rock to go to her and…you know. How's that gonna work?"

Louis lit another cigarette. He'd let me grab a bottle of Jack from the corner market and the first sip had burned sooooo good.

"All we need is a sentient spirit."

"Like a ghost?"

"Nah, mate. There are spirits all around us. Not all of them are human. They just exist. You ever see a statue and just think it's staring at you, even though you know it's not true? Ever feel like someone's creeping up behind you and it's only the breeze through a tree's leaves? You just have to know where to look."

As I tipped the bottle back and looked toward the sky, I found our spirit.

Chapter Five

The best part about being a gargoyle is the vantage point. For example, on this particular evening, the night sky was clear, the lights were bright, and the redhead in the apartment across the street from me was taking a bath.

Ah, yes. Gingers. That creamy skin...the freckles... I sometimes imagined that I had real fingers and I could play connect-the-dots with a willing participant. Not like those jerks in the parties upstairs from her. Alas, I was stuck in place high above the city street. I had great vision though. I watched this beautiful woman recline in the tub, my stony parts getting a bit warm...

I watched people, what of it? It's lonely up here above the city. I don't remember how it all started, or how I came to be. I'm just a rock that can see, hear and think for itself. Remember that, next time you pick one up and chuck it.

My stony parts were getting warmer watching the redhead lather her lovely skin, and as her hand dipped beneath the surface, her head tilted back over the ledge of the tub and her lips—

"Ya perv! You know you could get ground up into asphalt, you keep that shit up."

I rolled my eyeballs around in their sockets and saw this guy with a big chip on his shoulder and a bigger gut sitting on my ledge with a bottle of Jack Daniel's. He looked like he smelled really bad. I could only imagine, since rocks can't smell. I'm not fully sentient. Thank goodness.

"What do you know about it?" I asked the guy. "And how did you know what I was doing?"

"Who *wouldn't* be staring at those tits?"

"Hey, watch your mouth, fat man! What are you doing on my ledge, anyway? It's not like there's an easy access point this far up."

The guy shrugged, and that's when I noticed that below his wife beater tank top, he was wearing some sort of coveralls and boots. He had the kind of body that you knew at one point had been at the pinnacle of physical fitness. Not so much now.

"What kind of getup is that?"

The dude looked down at his gear and shrugged again. He took a tug on the bottle and burped loudly.

"I'm a goddamned fireman, that's what I am. And you're a piece of shit, Rock Boy. Neither of us belong up here, so fuck it. I'm getting drunk!"

"You already are drunk. And you're ruining my fantasy, coming up here with your flatulence and bad aura. This is all I got, man!"

The guy turned to look at me. "Oh, a fantasy. You want a fantasy? What if I told ya I could give you that fantasy?"

Who the hell was this guy? "Yeah. Right. What're you gonna do, puke on me? Show me your junk? That's no fantasy. That's a nightmare."

"You asked why I'm up here. Well, I'm afraid of heights."

How much dumber could this guy get? Wait, I shouldn't ask that.

"That makes loads of sense. Now, can you leave me—"

"I gotta drink or I can't be up here. See, I'm Father Christmas, and—"

"Oh wow, drunk and delusional. Look, man, I don't know what—"

"Let me finish, dumbass, or you won't get your wish! Now, I was a firefighter. I died, alright? And when I got to the afterlife, they asked me what I wanted to do with myself. Being the asshole I am, I said 'Make me fucking Santa Claus!' And you know what that old lady in the gymnasium said? 'That position is already taken, but if you would like to grant Christmas miracles, you may become a Father Christmas representative. It will be your job to grant wishes to those deserving them in the weeks before Christmas.' Sounded better than sitting around on my ass, so I says, sure. How bad could it be? Rule a' thumb: Don't ever ask that question!"

The guy got quiet for a bit and I decided to humor him. "Father fuckin' Christmas, eh? Well. If you're really Father Christmas, make me a man so I can go on over to that high-rise and make sweet love to that redhead right there in the tub. Oh, and you'll probably have to make me all magical, so she won't freak out if I barge in on her while she's all soapy and wet."

There was no way what he was saying was true, and I had nothing else to do but mess with him and hope I didn't have to watch him jump and splatter himself all over the ground below. I'd seen that enough times, thank you very much. I always tried to talk them down. I did. I hated to see people throw it all away because life seemed tough at the time.

Sometimes I succeeded and they left to go about their lives. The worst, though, was the time this woman climbed out the window below my ledge with her kid. I begged and pleaded, the kid held on for all his might when his mom tried to pull him out the window and over the ledge with her. Poor little fella. She fell, but someone reached out and grabbed him at the last minute, thank God. I would have hated to see the little guy go that way.

His mom caused a helluva car wreck.

I got lost in my thoughts for a few minutes and didn't realize the guy had scooted closer.

"You're still here?" I asked him, wondering what sort of nonsense he'd spew next. Just words, hopefully. Puke was nasty, no matter if I was a piece of stone. At least I couldn't smell it, but my eyes and ears work just perfectly.

"I am. Make up your mind. You want a woman? I'll make it happen. You'll have this entire night to live as a man with the perfect woman."

He seemed to sober up with that statement. He frowned at the building across from us and took another swig from his bottle, letting out a coughing gasp at the burn.

"Sure," I said, wishing again he'd just go away. "You do that. Just don't pass out up here, all right? The last drunk who climbed out here, crying about losing his job, passed out and splatted on the street below. I really hate that."

"Fine, whatever. All right. Just close your eyes and picture what you want to look like and what you want to happen. I gotta see it in my mind, this thing I do where I see… Never mind. Close 'em."

I closed my eyes and chuckled to myself. What a joke! I tried to think about people I'd seen. Definitely not the jerk in the penthouse or any of his loser friends.

It took a moment before I got just the right ridiculous thought in my head: Who better for me to turn into but that actor I'd seen, Dwayne "The Rock" Johnson? What woman would turn me away from her door?

"Alright. I got it," I said to the guy, hoping he'd realize his hocus pocus was ridiculous and he'd leave me alone. The redhead would be out of the tub soon.

The guy placed his hand on my head and he was quiet. I heard him take a deep breath and then I felt… Heat. It got hot where his hand was…

I opened my eyes to tell the guy to shove off—and everything had changed.

Instead of being on my ledge? I was standing on the street below.

What the ever-loving hell?

A car horn honked and a guy dressed all in green and wearing a Santa hat leaned out the window.

"Merry fuckin' Christmas, asshole!"

I returned his middle finger salute and shook my head. This city was such a trip. People could be celebratory and dickish in the same breath.

I caught my reflection in the window of a car parked on the street. I was now an exact copy of Dwayne Johnson, but not. There were some differences in the face and smile, just enough to throw people. *Whoa.*

Before me was a nearly deserted street and the doors to the redhead's building. All I needed to do was cross the street, take the elevator up to the 36th floor, and then her door was halfway down the hall. Piece of cake.

I rubbed my gigantic hands together and looked down to inspect them. *Holy shit.* And the muscled forearms that led to massive biceps… Then I looked down past hugenormous pecs to gigantor thighs… I was The Rock. The real Rock, not just a stupid decoration on a building. And I had all night to finally live out all of my carnal fantasies. All I had to do was cross that street without becoming roadkill.

I looked both ways, because that's what I always heard parents telling their kids to do, and when I didn't see any cars, I jogged across and hopped up the steep curb to the sidewalk. These damn legs were so strong. I felt as if I could jump as high as the 36th floor. But then, I wanted to experience the inside of the building for once, not just see the outside.

I entered the lobby through the circular door and caught the notice of a few people hanging out. Some guys were with dates, all dressed up fancy. This place was classy. Luckily when

Father fuckin' Christmas transformed me, he put me in a suit, or I might stand out.

Who was I kidding? I was a massive guy who looked like Dwayne Johnson. I was going to stand out in San Francisco or anywhere I was.

I somehow knew just where the elevator was, so I crossed the lobby, being sure to greet everyone with Johnson's signature eyebrow raise. As I climbed in, two women were just exiting. They turned around, gasping and giggling, trying to figure out if I was really the famous actor. I made my pec muscles pop for them and winked as the doors closed.

Okay, by now, you're probably wondering how I know so much about this actor. Well, the woman who lives next door to the hot redhead watches his movies nearly 24/7. I'd seen them all. She never really went anywhere, just took care of a herd of cats, so it was all Dwayne, all the time. He was the quintessential hero in my eyes.

The elevator doors opened on the 36th floor, and I suddenly felt something weird going on in my midsection. Now, I'd never been in a human body before, so I had no clue what the midsection should feel like, but since I hadn't felt it outside on the street, it had to have something to do with being near the redhead. Excitement. Nerves. Anticip-p-p...ation.

Yeah, that was another movie the crazy chick next door played on repeat. *The Rocky Horror Picture Show*. I had to admit I loved the music. I looked down at this body I was in and chuckled, imagining Dwayne Johnson wearing that corset-and-garters getup.

Enough. It was time to claim my woman. Or the woman of my lewd fantasies. Or… Oh man, this sounded all perverted-like. I would just walk down the hall, knock on the door halfway down, and when she didn't open it, since she was probably still in the bathtub, I'd open the door, waltz right in the bathroom, and give her —

What? What exactly would I do? I really hadn't thought this through, and now I was standing in front of her door. What if she screamed? What if she called the cops? What if…

Nope. The Rock did not shy from a challenge. Ever. If I'd learned anything from watching all of his movies, I knew he always got the girl. Except in *The Rundown*. Which was fine, she was a badass anyway. That was my favorite.

I turned to face her door, my hands shaking for some reason. The Rock never got nervous.

My hand turned into a beefy fist and banged loudly on the door, startling me. I heard a shriek on the other side of the door.

"Great, Romeo. Way to scare the lady," I muttered.

I posed in front of the door, making sure all of my muscles were standing at attention, and I perked up that eyebrow, ready to take —

The door flew open and I instantly realized my mistake.

The woman before me gasped, her eyes growing enormous behind her thick glasses. She had a purple towel wrapped around her hair. White flannel pajamas with flying cows on them peeked out from beneath a pink, fuzzy robe, and her feet were ensconced in slippers with huge reindeer heads on top of them.

My eyes traveled back up her body, and before I knew it, she'd grabbed me by my beefy arm and dragged me into her apartment, slamming the door behind me with a sort of finality.

"When that English guy told me you'd show up, I totally didn't believe him, otherwise I'd be dressed for this, but you're really here!"

She squealed once more and dragged me over to the couch, where she promptly pushed me down.

"Don't go away," she threatened as she scurried into the next room.

One of her cats hopped up onto the arm of the sofa and meowed at me.

Pet me scratch me love me.

I tried to look intimidating, but it stepped a tentative paw onto my chest and rubbed its head on my jaw, purring loudly.

It was bizarre, seeing the apartment from inside. I turned and looked out the window over at my building, and sure enough, my gargoyle self was still perched, staring creepily at me. There was no drunken fireman.

"Can I get you something to drink, Mr. Johnson?" she called out.

"Oh, I'm not Dwayne Johnson. My name is—"

"He told me you would say you weren't Dwayne Johnson. I honestly don't care. You're here, and that's all that matters," she said, now standing in the doorway.

My jaw dropped in shock. The goofy getup was gone. Now she was wearing a slinky green dress that hung to just above her knees and sort of wrapped around her, leaving a gap between her... *Oh.* Her hair was pulled up into a damp, loose bun on top of her head, and she'd removed her glasses.

In the place of the crazy cat lady now stood the most beautiful creature I'd ever seen in the many years I'd perched atop the high-rise. Her eyes were as blue as the bluest skies over the San Francisco Bay, and her teeth sparkled like those of the models in the toothpaste ads they placed on the billboards near the 80 freeway. I couldn't believe this was the same woman.

Speaking of cats, another one chose this moment to attempt to climb onto my lap like the damn thing was climbing a mountain.

You're in my spot, asshole.

I cursed and stood hurriedly, but that only made the thing dig its claws into my leg deeper, shredding the material of my pants with each movement.

"No! Derek, you let go right now!"

"Derek? The cat's name is Derek?"

She grinned as she took another cat off of the seat I'd just vacated so I wouldn't squish it with my huge mass when I sat down.

"Well sure! Your character in the *Tooth Fairy* movie was named Derek! We've also got Hank from *Journey 2: The Mysterious Island,* Elliot Wilhelm from *Be Cool,* and, my favorite," she leaned in and whispered closely on this last one.

"Beck from *The Rundown*. Sarge and Danson are in the other room. You know, from *Doom* and *The Other Guys*?"

This woman really knew her Dwayne Johnson movies.

"Yeah, well, that's great and all, but I'm not really—"

She pushed up on her tiptoes and pressed her lips insistently against mine. Her hand snaked around my neck and she held on tight. My eyes remained open while my body went into what I assumed was sheer panic mode.

She kissed me.

What was I supposed to do with that? Sure, I'd seen the Dwayne Johnson movies, but things never really got that hot and heavy. All I knew about touching and kissing a woman came from the porn the guys in the penthouse watched, or what I'd seen in the apartment below, but that wasn't exactly going to help me now. That probably wasn't the way to go with the crazy cat lady.

I gripped her waist and set her back on her feet. "I wasn't expecting anything like this to happen."

She blinked and took a step back. "I'm sorry. I knew this was a bad idea."

I couldn't stand the sadness in her eyes. "No, I didn't mean it was bad, just... Hi, I'm gar— Garth. Stone. Garth Stone." I reached out my hand to shake hers like I'd seen people do on the street.

Her tentative grip in my hand sent a shiver up my arm. She was so soft compared to this body I now inhabited. I tugged her hand, perhaps a little harder than I should have, and she crashed against my massive chest. Her blue eyes were so deep, I couldn't help staring.

"He said you would come," she said. "And that I would have one night with you. I didn't want to ruin it by talking. Most men think I'm boring or that I talk too much or—"

"I like talking. I don't get to talk to people much, only if they're trying to jump off my building or—"

"Oh! You mean like when you save people from killing themselves? Like in your movie?"

"No, I'm not... I'm not really Dwayne Johnson. I just look like him. I guess."

I turned to look behind me at the mirror on her wall. The resemblance was close, but my eyes were gray. I remember from the films that the real Johnson had dark brown eyes. And there were other subtle differences...

"Well whoever you are, the guy said I'd only have tonight, so we should probably go into the bedroom."

My attention snapped back to her. "The bedroom? But we don't have to..."

Her eyes flared and she smiled. The innocent cat lady was gone. A vixen took her place. "Oh, but we *do*!"

And then she jumped on me, her legs straddling my waist, and whatever it is that makes a man, um, excited, happened. Intensely. I felt something *growing* until I thought it would split the pants open in front.

Cat lady kissed me until I couldn't breathe, and I didn't care one bit.

"Wait," I said, trying to catch my breath. She ran her tongue down my throat and I almost dropped her, I was shaking so hard. "What's your name?"

"Kimberly Quintana. I work at the Animal Care and Control Center. I love cats. Now can we do it?"

We were gonna do *something*. She pointed me in the direction of her bedroom and I started to walk, but I heard a shriek.

Watch your step, you giant piece of meat!

I wonder when she's going to feed us again?

Do you think she got that fancy food again? That stuff gave me the squirts.

"What was that?"

I couldn't look where I was walking at all. She looked down and laughed. "Oh, Elliot! You better move!" Her kisses covered every inch of my face, and I was enjoying the feel of her thighs in my hands so much, I didn't think about what I'd just heard. She gripped me with her legs as I began to move again, taking careful steps this time to avoid stepping on her cats, who were now meowing loudly.

As we entered the bedroom, I walked forward until I kicked the bedframe, bruising my shin. I grunted and she pulled away, gasping.

"Sorry. I should have warned you." She let her legs untangle and knelt on the bed. A cat screeched and jumped out of the way. She pulled off my suit jacket and lifted my white t-shirt over my head. Her delicate hands began working the fly of my pants.

I looked around and blanched. Feline eyes tracked our movements curiously. Two more cats jumped onto the bed from the bookshelf and walked toward us.

This is getting good.

I hope she doesn't bring out that loud buzzing thing again.

"Um, Kimberly?"

"Hmmm? Oh! You boys!" She shooed the cats off the bed and out the door, closing it behind her. When she turned back to face me, she growled before charging me and tackling me on the bed. She landed on top and straddled my chest. She pulled her dress up over her head and I groaned at the sight of her lacy underthings. Her creamy skin was even softer than I'd imagined, so lovely.

I ran my hands everywhere I could reach, telling her over and over how beautiful she was. How lovely she smelled. I could actually smell! It was heavenly, as if she'd rubbed flowers on her skin.

She threw her head back and dug her nails into my chest.

"I want to do it just like this." She moved to the side and wiggled out of her panties and unhooked her bra before climbing back into position. She stared down at me as she pulled on her nipples, making them stand at attention.

I couldn't believe this was really happening. My pants and shoes were still on and I couldn't reach them with her on top of me. I went to move her, but we ended up rolling together. Once she was beneath me, I took my time exploring her. If this was going to be my only time, I wanted to enjoy it.

She yanked at my pants, cursing when she couldn't get them off.

"Hey, it's okay. We don't have to hurry. I don't *want* to hurry," I admitted.

"But I don't know when you're going to be gone, and I just want..."

"Why? You're such a beautiful woman. Why would you—"

"Because I don't want to go my whole life without having sex again!"

Her hair was wild, as were her eyes. She looked so vulnerable under my giant hands. I took a moment to smooth back her hair. Her eyes closed and she took in a deep breath.

"When the Christmas Wish guy came into the shelter, he said he could offer me a wish, that I'd earned it. He somehow knew about my husband, how he died fighting a fire, and how I'd been alone for a really long time. I love my husband," she choked out, tears streaming down her face now. "But he's gone. The guy said I deserved to be happy, I just had to imagine it. The only other man I ever thought about was The Rock, and I thought that was too silly, but he was all I could think of. I know I could never be with another *real* man, you know? And then you showed up at my door!"

She looked confused and unsure. She tried to reach for the bathrobe she'd laid across the end of the bed. I stopped her.

"Please don't cover yourself. Please. I don't know what's happening here, why I'm here, why he sent me to you, but I want to do this right."

There had to be a reason the drunk guy sent me to her. I looked through the window and across to my old building. My stony prison remained, staring at me through blank eyes. There had to be a reason this was all happening. It had to be right.

I lowered myself carefully onto her body and captured her lips in a deep kiss. I tried not to think about what happened in the porn movies and figured if I could just go slow and try to make her feel good, maybe I wouldn't totally mess up.

So that's what I did. I went slow. I touched her everywhere and learned to tell the difference between the frustrated moans and the excited moans, and the *"Oh God!"* moans. Those were my favorites. I made her moan like that over and over while I used the shit out of this body I'd been given. It was certainly made for making a woman moan, and I enjoyed it a whole helluva lot.

Her smile after we'd finished told me I did good.

We lay together for a long time, trying to catch our breath. I thought she was sleeping, but then she rolled over and I heard a tiny quiver in her voice.

"I miss you, Tommy," she whispered.

A moment later, she snored loudly.

I heard scratching sounds at the door and figured her feline friends were not pleased to be kept out. I climbed out of bed, trying not to disturb her, angry to be leaving her side at all. I never wanted to leave her side. If this was what humans got to experience, even just once in a while, it would be worth it. To share this experience with another and to be in love…

I slid the pants back on and opened the door to let the cats in. And realized we weren't alone.

Chapter Six

"You're not looking too hot, mate. That was a good thing you done, eh? I bet it's something terrible to watch your old lady with another? Specially one who looked like that bloke—"

"Shut up already, ya limey bastard. You're damn right it don't feel good." This fucking asshole with the Mohawk's gonna come in here and tell me...

My Kimberly. Why did I have to go and fuck things up so bad?

We had plans, me and Kimberly. We were gonna have kids. She wanted a whole bunch of them, but I kept putting her off, thinking I wasn't ready. We were saving up to go on a cruise and I thought we could try then. We even started looking at houses. All that changed when I had my first incident. I was a total dick to her that last year. I threw away perfection.

I wanted to make it right, and not just for one night. She deserved better.

I couldn't figure out how to get the actual Dwayne Johnson to hook up with her, so Louis had said we could find a spirit trapped in an inanimate object, and I gave it a shot. Besides, when I got to that ledge, I could see how bad the guy was jonesin' to get laid. How'd you like to be hard as stone forever without no way to get your rocks off?

Heh heh, gargoyle humor, I guess.

I should have stayed away, but I'd been curious. Would he be gentle? Would he take care of her? She seemed happy when he took her back to the bedroom, but I'd heard her crying in the end.

"I miss you, Tommy."

How could I give her this night and then take it all away?

"Lemme ask you something. Is that it? Now that she got laid, she's just going to bounce right back and start over? Is that how it works? Cuz I know my Kimberly. She ain't gonna run off with no fucking guy just because a' this. She thinks this is all made up. Well, it *is* made up. I don't want her to be alone, you get what I'm sayin'?"

"This was our intervention, mate. This was all we were meant to do. We cannot interfere more or we run the risk of—"

"Oh, fuck the risk! I want her to be happy! She doesn't deserve to be a fuckup's widow!"

I buried my face in my hands and felt tears coming on. They weren't like the drunk tears that wreck ya but you don't remember them when you're through. These were the kinda tears that ripped your heart in two and you felt them forever.

"If you do anything further, you risk giving up your eternal peace."

I thought long and hard. I'd been a pretty good Catholic, at least until I hit high school and started banging all the chicks behind St. Luke's. But we all did that. I thought by becoming a fireman and saving people, I'd get some redemption. But now, seeing the fucking Rock look-alike leave Kimberly's bedroom, seeing her curled up with tears drying on her face, I knew I wouldn't ever have no peace if I left it like this.

So I prayed. I turned my face up to the heavens and thanked the Holy Spirit for giving me a girl like Kimberly, and I made my choice.

"I'll give anything to see her happy and taken care of."

Louis swore under his breath. "You're serious? You'd give up peace? You have no idea what this existence is like. The constant wandering, seeing other people find their happiness. A lot of them fuck it up worse, you listening to what I'm telling you? You could give up your peace and she could still end up—"

"I owe her."

Louis lit a cigarette and took a long drag. "Right. Well, you've made your choice. Grandma will let you know what's what when we return. You just better be careful what you agree to."

The bedroom door opened wider and out stepped the massive dude. He'd pulled on his pants, but his chest was still bare. As much as I wanted to hate him, he just oozed this innocence and goodness. If it were anyone else, I'd give him shit about it. But not this time. This time, the joke was on me.

Chapter Seven

"What happens now?" I asked Father Christmas. The guy rubbed a hand down his face and stood from the couch. As he approached, a grim determination seemed to come over him. He stood an inch or so shorter than my enormous self and pointed a finger in my chest, poking me hard.

"What happens now is you fuckin' take care a' that woman. She's yours. Don't make me regret givin' her to you, ya hear me?"

He turned for the door, shoulders hunched low.

What did he mean?

"Wait! When do I return to my ledge?"

"You don't," he said without turning around. His hand was on the doorknob. "I don't know what to tell you. I don't know what's going to happen. But you get to stay with her. That's the deal I'm making. Just take care of her. Give her babies, for Christ's sake, so she quits bringing home these damn cats."

He shook his head and opened the door. I noticed another man stood with him, a skinny-looking guy with a black

Mohawk and gray eyes. He smoked a cigarette and looked disgusted with the world.

"You've got everything you need to start your life in that wallet there," the Mohawk guy said, gesturing with his head towards me, "and, well, you'll figure out the rest."

I felt a weight in the back of the pants that hadn't been there before. I reached down and pulled out a leather wallet. Inside, I found a driver's license with the name Garth Stone on it. The address listed was some place in Oakland. Credit cards, a thick wad of cash.

But how? Was this even possible?

"What he didn't tell you," the Mohawk guy continued, 'is that you only have until Christmas Eve. That's the best I can arrange. You have to make her fall for you by then, or else..." He looked between the drunk fireman and me as if to say more. He nodded to me once, and I felt a blast of heat push me backwards as the door slammed shut.

"What was that?" Kimberly hurried to my side, wrapping her robe around her. "Was someone here, Garth?"

I looked down at her, all disheveled from sleep. My chest felt like a bomb went off in it. This woman was mine now. She belonged to me. This time, The Rock got the girl, because this rock wasn't a fantasy, he was the real thing, and he was going to make this woman incredibly happy for the rest of her life.

Right. And how, exactly?

"Just the firemen doing a safety check on the building."

She grinned at me shyly, pressing up on her toes to give me a sleepy kiss. "I'm sorry. For what I—"

"I understand. He was your husband. You loved him."

She nodded, looking toward a picture of him on the shelf. "I miss a version of him. The one from before... He wasn't the same man when he died. He'd had an accident at work and then he started drinking... I just wanted him to be happy."

I took a closer look at the shelf and realized that—holy shit! The drunk guy was her husband. He looked like shit now, but I could definitely see what she'd loved about him. In the picture, he smiled down at her like she was a true thing to be worshipped, like he was the luckiest sonofabitch on the planet.

"He wants you to be happy," I murmured.

Kimberly gazed up at me, wide-eyed.

"What did you just say?"

"I said he'd want you to be happy." I couldn't afford to slip like that.

Her eyes narrowed and she shook her head. "He sure as hell wouldn't have wanted some other guy touching me. He wasn't like super jealous, but I knew. I'd just hoped to have time to help him get better, to make him see how much of a hero he really was."

She shuddered and took in a deep breath. "Doesn't matter now. You're still here, and it's not tomorrow yet. I say we eat, then we go back to bed. I'm not done with you tonight."

Her words sounded more confident than she looked. She wandered into the kitchen, kind of stumbling along like she'd been drinking.

"What do you say? Want me to make us some omelets? Is that kinda cliché? I swear in all the movies, they have omelets after sex or something. I got some pasta."

I followed her into the kitchen, her scent beckoning to me more than the idea of food.

"We could always have porcini mushrooms."

She gave me a confused look. What did I know about food? I just remembered The Rock making a list at the beginning of *The Rundown*. He was writing down some sort of recipe…

"Whatever you have will be fine."

We ended up eating Hot Pockets she found in her freezer. Apparently, she wasn't a huge fan of cooking, said she made huge meals for her husband and his family, even though she hated cooking. Turned out she did a lot of things she hated because it made him happy. I was glad the drunk was gone or I might have been tempted to slap him.

"I'm sorry, I should have made something nice for you after all you did," she said with a shy smile. She crossed her legs and squirmed in her seat, her cheeks red.

"After all *I* did?" I reached across her tiny table and linked fingers with her. "I seem to recall you being a very active participant."

I loved the contrast of our skin tones and the size of my giant fingers twirling with her dainty ones. Her nails were short and neat. Her long hair fell in waves and a shorter piece in front hung over one eye. I remembered she'd worn it pulled back all of the previous times I'd seen her going to and returning from work. The way it fell around her face tonight…

"I've always enjoyed sex," she said in a quiet voice. "I know that's weird. Women aren't supposed to like it, or something. But I always did. Tommy…" She paused and made a face. "My ex. He used to tease me about how much I liked it. Then I'd get embarrassed, and then he'd tell me it was okay and then we'd do it and then he'd tease me. It was kind of this stupid game we played."

How did I respond to that with my limited experience? Easy. I would just say the first thing that popped in my head.

"He was stupid, then. Why shouldn't you enjoy it? Maybe he wasn't doing it right."

She had been drinking milk, and she coughed as I spoke, shooting the liquid all over the table. I jumped up to grab a towel at the same time she jumped up, but my movement was more disastrous as I managed to flip her little table over with my big body. Milk from her glass went everywhere, including all over her robe. I still had mine in my hand. Before I knew it, there were cats flocking to the kitchen in droves, licking up the spill.

Milk milk milk milk milk.

No need to shove, there's plenty for everyone.

"Well, at least someone benefitted from this mess," she said with a frown.

I had to salvage the moment. I took my glass of milk I'd managed to rescue and I poured it over myself.

"There. We're even."

She snorted, looked at me as if I was crazy. Maybe I was, I could almost swear I heard the cats talking. That wasn't normal, right?

I dabbed some milk on her nose. She sputtered in shock, kind of adorably. I couldn't resist. I picked up a bowl of sugar she had next to a container of teabags on her counter and I flung the sugar at her.

She held up her hands but she was laughing hysterically. She backed away from the table toward the fridge.

"So this is how you like to play, huh?" She turned and reached inside.

Next thing I knew, I heard a cracking sound and cold goo ran down my chest. She pointed and threw her head back, laughing even harder. Another egg hit me in the chest and that was it. I stalked over to her and caged her in with my body. She stared up at me, her eyes wide as though she wasn't sure I was still playing. I gave her my best Dwayne Johnson glare.

"You've got two choices. Option A, you give me the eggs. Option B, I make you give me the eggs. You should really take Option A."

With a serious look on her face, she reached inside the refrigerator, her eyes never leaving mine, and grabbed another egg. I watched as she slowly brought the egg towards me and smashed it on my chest. By now my skin was sticky and stiff from the eggs, but I was enjoying this too much.

"You really should have taken Option A." I poured the entire box of cereal that was on top of the fridge over her head.

Rice Krispies. She squealed as the little puffs clung to her everywhere.

"I tried to be reasonable," I said as I claimed her mouth in a kiss. I slid the bathrobe from her shoulders and it landed with a splat on the floor. I greedily ran my hands over her skin, now covered in bumps from the chill of the cool air from the refrigerator. I ran my tongue along her neck, catching a few of the rice puffs as I went.

"If you wanted cereal, I could have just poured you a bowl," she panted.

"This is much better."

I wanted to get her horizontal again, desperate to be inside her once more, so I picked her up and sat her on the island in her small kitchen. She giggled as I pushed her onto her back and ran my hands between her breasts. This body knew exactly what to do with the gorgeous woman before me. I didn't want the cereal to scratch her perfect skin, so I brushed it off with a towel before using my tongue to finish cleaning her off. I enjoyed it so much, I continued moving lower, and lower...

I heard her curse just as her hands moved my head exactly where she needed me to be. I continued using my tongue to gain the upper hand.

Sex in her kitchen was even more fun than the bedroom, and she responded enthusiastically. She knocked the fruit bowl onto the floor when she came; apples, bananas and oranges bounced on the floor, gathering at my feet. Before the shudders had finished working their way through her body, she sat up and yanked on the front of my pants, unfastening them with a whimper.

"Now, Garth. I need you *now!*"

I was all too happy to comply. The island was the perfect height, her core was wonderfully accommodating, and the grip of her thighs provided a fantastic counterbalance as I gave her everything I could. When I thought I'd experienced all the bliss I'd be allowed, she sat up, threw her arms around my neck and kissed me deeply. She sucked my tongue into her mouth, and that was it for me. My whole body seized up in complete ecstasy and I shouted hoarsely as I released into her beautiful body. I continued to rock into her involuntarily, as though my body never wanted this sensation to end.

"That," I finally said, "was the most amazing experience. I don't ever want to leave this spot right here."

"I may not be able to. My ass is stuck to the counter," she said with a laugh. She reached behind me and squeezed my ass, pulling me deeper into her and putting me off balance. I moved my foot to center myself and felt something squish between my toes.

"Ewwwww," I groaned.

Kimberly looked down and giggled. "Be careful. You're standing on a banana peel. You slip on a banana peel and you'll fall—"

"For you."

Her eyes widened in surprise.

"Garth—"

"I have. I've fallen for you. I want more than just tonight. I want—"

She shook her head. "No." She pushed back from me, the sound of her skin unsticking from the counter was cringeworthy. "We only had tonight. And it's morning."

Sure enough, one glance at the clock showed it was near five o'clock. Dawn would come soon.

Kimberly hopped off the counter and continued mumbling under her breath.

"Kimberly—"

"No! We can't! I can't. I'm a married woman. You're a fantasy. You're not even real!"

I reached for her hand and placed it on my chest. "I'm real, alright. He made me real, for you. He—"

She tried to pull her hand back, but it stuck to the egg. She peeled it off with a wince.

"I'm sorry. I don't know what's happening here, but this was supposed to be for one night. I never would have agreed. As much as he was a jerk at the end, I love my husband and our vows were forever. 'Til death do us part."

"And he's dead," I said, grasping her by the shoulders gently.

Rather than reassuring her, my words seemed to bring out her stubbornness. She crossed her arms over her chest and cocked a hip to the side.

"I made a promise, and I keep my promises." A single tear rolled down her cheek. "Thank you for tonight, but you need to leave."

She turned and scurried from the kitchen, leaving me with my pants around my ankles, surrounded by staring cats, and with egg and food everywhere. One of the cats, Derek I think, approached me.

Don't leave.

He meowed, placed his front paw on my thigh and batted with the other one, coming dangerously close to—

"I don't think so," I said, hopping out of reach. That hop, combined with the placement of another banana, had me on my ass. Hard.

So much for Christmas miracles...

Chapter Eight

By the time the sun began to light up the sky, a rarity for a San Francisco morning, I'd cleaned up the last of our mess and was headed out the door. I took a chance to glance in on her once more. She'd showered, and from the number of wadded-up tissues and the empty box next to her on the bed, she'd cried herself to sleep again.

I made sure to lock up behind me as I begrudgingly shut her apartment door. Whatever was inside my chest, whether it was a true human heart, or something entirely different, it felt like it was breaking.

It was as though this little "intervention" or whatever the drunk fireman, her husband Tommy, was up to, had just made things worse.

I spent the day wandering the city, ending up in Union Square surrounded by holiday shoppers. Christmas cheer was the last thing I needed.

Come here, you little bastard.

Walking past an alley, I heard a scuffle.

I need dinner! Get in my belly!

I took a few steps into the small space between the buildings and saw a scruffy-looking orange tabby cat, with chunks missing out of his ears, chasing a rat almost as big as him. The rat saw me first and dashed behind a Dumpster and into some sort of drain.

Motherfucker. You happy now? That was going to be an epic meal.

The cat and I stared at each other in surprise.

What the hell are you looking at, human?

"What are *you* looking at, furball?"

Holy shit. He can—

"Hear you. Yeah. What's going on?"

Beats me. Why don't you get the fuck out of here so the rat will come back? Homie's gotta eat, yo.

"Forgive me," I said, bowing to the cat. "I'm sorry to have messed up your dinner."

The cat flicked his chin at me and then promptly turned his ass in my direction. And sprayed. Thankfully, I was out of reach. I did interrupt his meal; however I didn't think that warranted a spraying.

But I could hear cats. This was not normal. I knew even though Kimberly talked to hers all the time, she didn't really *hear* them. They didn't talk *to* her.

They talked to me. A rock. Oh, the irony.

I passed an Asian restaurant and saw fish on their menu. I went inside and ordered a meal and returned to the alley.

"Hey asshole," I called out, setting the food a few feet inside the alley. "Sorry about the rat. I hope this makes up for it."

As I backed away, the cat stuck its head out from a pile of trash.

Did you bring me fish?

"Yeah. Sorry."

I turned to leave and heard a rustle of paper. The cat trotted over to the container of food and sniffed suspiciously. The heat must have caused him to jerk back a little.

Smells like heaven.

"If that's what heaven smells like," I answered with a laugh, "then I'd rather lose my sense of smell once again."

The cat just gave me a bored look then proceeded to scarf down the fish.

At least I did one good deed.

Thanks a lot. Now get the fuck out of here. I don't like being watched while I eat.

"Fine," I replied and turned from the alley. Poor guy. Hopefully he'd have a good day today.

I continued my observations, hoping I'd see something that would give me some clue as to how I could win Kimberly's love. I followed some women discreetly and tried to eavesdrop on their conversation, but if I got too close they'd turn, giggle, and move away. Sometimes looking like The Rock made it tough to just blend in.

One group of women, which appeared to be a mother and her adult daughters, discussed gifts they might get from their father.

"He always gets the same things. Scarves. Who wears scarves every day? Have I ever worn a scarf?"

"Well, you do at Christmas."

"I'm not trying to hurt the guy's feelings! Of course I'm going to wear his scarves."

"And therefore, you perpetuate the useless gifts."

"Mom, what does Dad get you?"

The older woman smiled.

"Oh, ew. I don't think we want to know."

When their mother didn't answer, just smiled as though she had a naughty secret, the three younger women began shrieking, shuddering and shouting, "ew!!! We don't need to know about that!"

"You asked," was all Mom replied.

They wandered off and I sighed. I was pretty sure I knew what Dad was giving Mom, and that hadn't done the trick with Kimberly.

I wound up in a giant department store called Bloomingdale's, watching a bunch of men hovering around the jewelry counter. The shopkeeper was rushing around to make sure every customer was helped.

I heard a familiar voice and turned to look back. I watched as the well-dressed man with the slick hairstyle and smile put a necklace on the woman who was teetering on tall wedge sandals, which I could properly identify after watching the redhead host clothing parties in her apartment. There was definitely something familiar about the guy, but I'd frankly never seen him in all of his clothes from my ledge.

It was the asshole from the penthouse. The life of the party. The biggest asshole.

I'd seen so much horrid behavior through his window, I couldn't imagine what this lovely woman was doing with him. It didn't seem right that he should have a beautiful woman on his arm when he was such a disgusting creature.

I couldn't let it go. As if on autopilot, I moved in their direction.

But then I paused. What the hell could I really do? Until yesterday I'd been a rock on top of a building. I had no idea how these things worked.

Wait. A rock. The Rock. What would The Rock do?

Before I knew what I was doing, my huge body stalked toward the laughing couple.

"Excuse me," I said, flashing my hugest smile. "Hi. I was just noticing that lovely pendant there. Is this your wife?" Innocent question.

The woman blushed and gazed up at the asshole as if she wished that was true. The asshole, on the other hand, experienced many feelings in the next ten seconds. Irritation at being interrupted, pleasure at the longing gaze from his woman, and fear at the fact that I'd moved a little closer and he came up to about my sternum.

"Do I know you?" He stepped back a bit from me, but I didn't let up on the pressure.

"Sure. I was at your party the other night. I thought we could have a conversation."

All attempts at keeping up appearances in front of the woman began crumbling. "Then you know we should be discussing these matters later." He grabbed the woman's arm and turned to go.

"Sir! Will you be purchasing the pendant?" The customer service representative in charge of the jewelry department blocked his path.

The man's eyes darted between the girl, the store employee, and me. Sweat broke out on his forehead.

He laughed nervously. It was a shrill sound, and his woman blanched as if thoroughly embarrassed by his behavior.

"Blake? What is going on here?"

"Uh, let me pay for this and we can be on our way, right?" The guy pulled out a black credit card and handed it to the store employee, who frowned and went back behind the counter.

"I'll just ring this up and then would you like me to gift wrap it, or will the lady be wearing it out of the store?"

The woman placed a possessive hand over her chest. "Oh, I'll be wearing it, thank you. Blake, I'm going to go look at the coats." She glanced between us curiously before sauntering off.

"I'm guessing she doesn't know about the parties? How silly, of course she doesn't, or she wouldn't be here, would she?"

Blake was in a world of hurt. He flinched when he glanced at the receipt.

"Fifty-three thousand dollars? Are you fucking—"

"Is there a problem?" the employee asked, looking annoyed with this whole scenario.

"Of course there isn't, is there, Blake? I'm sure fifty thousand is nothing for a big man like yourself."

He finished paying, and then Blake turned to face me, his cheeks mottled red with anger. "Look, I don't know who the fuck you are, and I sure as hell would never have you up to the penthouse, but you need to—"

"You've been under surveillance, Blake." Really? I supposed that was true. My mouth ran on ahead of me. "I'm sure there are all kinds of felonies we could be discussing: kidnapping, false imprisonment, statutory rape—well, rape period, seeing as many of those women, regardless of whether they were professionals or not, didn't seem happy when they ran out of your den of sin... Shall I go on?"

"I don't know what the fuck you're talking about, friend, but I'm going to leave now." Blake smirked before turning away.

I felt inexplicably angry all of a sudden and yet I kept my cool. Something compelled me into action. I grabbed him by the collar and yanked him off his feet like the puny little maggot he was.

"That was the wrong answer, Blake. Now, you and I are going to take a walk and discuss the parties, do you understand?"

I dropped him back to his feet and he immediately looked around, straightening his jacket. His woman was nowhere in sight, so he turned on me with fire in his eyes.

"And just what the fuck is it you want to discuss?"

I leaned in close, almost nose to nose with the sleazebag, and said, "You are going to quit with the parties. Now. Or I am going to the authorities. I know a few agencies who would be very interested in the cash flowing in and out of your hands."

I had no clue what I was saying, but the more I spoke, the wider his eyes grew and all the color drained from his face.

"You aren't serious. Do you know what will happen to me if the people I work for find out?"

"That's not my problem. You've dug your own grave, friend."

"Look, I'll do anything. Just let me disappear." The guy had grabbed the lapels of my jacket and was pleading with me. "They'll destroy me. Slowly. They'll find pieces of me in the Bay, especially if anyone finds out about the girls."

The girls? "You better show me what we're dealing with."

I was getting way deep in this situation, but the words kept pouring out of my mouth. Movement out of the corner of my eye helped to explain the situation. Louis and Tommy were standing off to the side. Louis was chuckling while Tommy watched with wide eyes, whispering to Louis. Louis nodded and I knew then where these words were coming from.

"You are going to hand them over to me, and you will pay a hefty sum to ensure they are well taken care of. And you are going to do all of this, Blake, with the understanding that at any moment I will signal to my friends with the FBI, who are standing by haul your ass to jail and make this all very, *very* public. What do you say? Shall we go back to your place?"

His beady eyes glanced around, and widened when he noticed two suited men with earpieces looking our way. The store employee must have called security when I got a little physical with the asshole, as they were keeping a close eye on us. Would he call my bluff?

"Fine," he said between clenched teeth. He threw his shoulders back. I kept a hand on his arm and nodded to the suits, who nodded back. I didn't know why they kept their distance, but I thought perhaps it was part of some divine intervention when I caught sight of a black Mohawk riding down the escalator.

Blake was cursing under his breath as we left the store and walked toward the parking garage. I had no idea where I was going, but he seemed to know. He pulled out his keys and I heard a chirp from off to the left. A ridiculously expensive sports car was parked in a spot near the back wall, and Blake moved toward it.

"I was just providing a service to some of my associates. The girls were taken care of, you know. I was just keeping them for a friend."

"Shut up, Blake. You are a disgusting human being. And if you make one stupid move between here and the penthouse, those guys in the store will be all over your ass since they're following close behind. You will release the girls and pay restitution. I better never hear of you doing this shit again, are we understood?" Somehow I knew instinctively what I should be doing in this situation so I went with it. I did what The Rock would have done.

"Yes," he said hoarsely.

"Good. Because not only will you be ruined financially, and your face plastered all over the world as a human trafficker, but I will personally be sure you disappear. Painfully." I cracked my knuckles for emphasis.

Honestly, I had no idea why this guy was doing anything I said. I was just following some sort of script in my head, probably from Louis's influence or maybe leftover from all the movies I'd watched through Kimberly's window.

Kimberly.

Chapter Nine

"What the fuck is he doing? This isn't part of the plan!" Rock Boy was supposed to be with Kimberly. What the hell had happened after we'd left them alone? All I could do was follow Louis around and watch helplessly.

Louis just smiled. "I thought I'd have a bit of fun with my next intervention, and wasn't that grand? Watching that bastard nearly piss himself in Bloomies?"

"Your next intervention?" I had no clue what the fuck Pin Cushion was talking about, but he was right. It served that fuckwad right, and watching our boy Stone pick him up effortlessly off the ground had been fan-fucking-tastic.

"Yeah. I needed to get those girls free of that cockwomble. As an Intervention Specialist, sometimes I actually get to save lives, isn't that just the cat's pajamas? One of the girls that bloke's been hiding has something very important to do, and who better to free her than an action hero look-alike hell-bent on justice? Just like the movies, isn't it?"

Once they got back to Kimberly's building, Stone went up to the penthouse with the Blake guy, me and Louis hot on their heels. Blake entered a code to open the door, which I noticed Stone paid close attention to, and led him inside. The place was a disaster, like they'd been having a massive party the night before. Blake turned to Garth with an angry look.

"So now what?"

"Now, you let the girls go, and you provide enough money to get them transported back to their families. I've seen enough depravity in this place to have you locked up for several lifetimes, since you've been under surveillance."

"Surveillance," I snorted. "That what you call being watched by a rock?"

Stone looked my way with a frown and Louis told me to hush.

"Let's not ruin the moment," Louis murmured, an evil glint of mischief in his eyes.

"How do you know these girls have some place to go back to?" Blake was backing away from Stone, who followed closely. He watched Blake's moves carefully, as though he anticipated the man would try to flee. He opened the first door and two girls squinted against the light.

"You sonofabitch," Stone growled. "How many?"

Blake's sweaty hand slipped off the keypad on the next door. "Six. I'm just holding them for a colleague. They're Russian, I guess. From somewhere over there. I didn't ask too many questions."

He opened two more doors, and Stone coaxed the girls out into the hallway. My humor over this jackass's behavior fled. Shit just got real. Stone looked as though he were ready to beat the life out of Blake. The girls looked frightened to death, as if they thought they were going from hell to a much worse place.

"I don't have a ton of cash on me, maybe two hundred thou? If you want more than that—"

"You'll be giving more. For now, it's a start. My associates will be in touch to determine your restitution."

Blake entered another room, this one an office, and pressed a button under the desk. A panel popped open on the wall and Blake entered a code into it. A safe door swung open with a beep, and inside were several stacks of cash.

"Take it all," he said, moving away towards his desk chair.

"Don't mind if we do," a British accented-voice spoke.

Louis had made himself visible, his Mohawk slicked down on his head and shitty punk rock clothes gone. He was now dressed quite snappily in a black suit with a black tie. He walked over to safe and grabbed two large stacks of cash, slipping them into an interior pocket on his coat. Blake stared blankly at him.

"Who the hell are you?"

Louis raised an eyebrow at him, and just like that, Blake blinked and fell down into a chair, fast asleep.

"Right. Now, if you lovely ladies will just follow me. Mr. Stone, I'll be taking it from here."

The girls glanced at each other, unsure what was going on.

"What will you do?" Stone asked him.

"I'll be taking them to the Russian consulate, where they will tell their tale to the authorities and pimp daddy dumbarse over here will be arrested shortly after. And since Blake here has signed over the place to you, my friend, you are now the proud owner of all this magnificence."

Stone looked around. "The penthouse? But how? Why?"

Louis shrugged. "Can't think of a better way for you to keep watch over the city. You just might come in handy if I have another intervention that requires your, ahem, skill set."

"Well I'll be damned," I said. "I can see now why that old lady said you were the best."

That cocky English bastard bowed with a wink. "At your service. Come then, ladies. Let's get you back home."

The girls stared blankly at him.

"Oh, right. Er, *poshli domoy.*"

The girls giggled at his behavior and followed him out.

"I'll be back for you, Fire Boy," Louis called before the last girl exited the door.

"Can you believe that shit?" I asked Stone. But his attention was elsewhere. It was sunset over the city, and the last of the sun's rays were shining down on his former perch. Garth gazed at the gargoyle staring back at him, and Garth had a sad expression on his face.

"Wishing you could go back? This world's pretty fucked, ain't it?"

He dropped down into a chair and put his head in his hands. "I honestly have no idea what to do," he said quietly.

I sat across from him, wondering how one goes about giving another guy pointers on wooing the woman the first guy is in love with.

"I take it all did not go well with Kimberly?"

He shook his head without looking up. "She says she's your wife. 'Til death. Yours, apparently, wasn't enough."

"She always was a stubborn broad. Look, I don't know what to tell you, but you have to win her over somehow. Louis said she—" I couldn't bring myself to utter the words. "You just have to."

"I don't know what to do! She wanted me gone this morning. I thought maybe I should buy her expensive jewelry, but that didn't seem right. I listened to women talk, and besides hearing some girls gross out over what their dad is giving their mom—"

"I'm not sure I really want to hear all this. Look, I didn't appreciate Kimberly enough, that's the God's honest truth, so don't take my word for it. I know she wanted kids, I know she wanted to save all the fuckin' cats in the damn city. That's all I got."

Garth sat back in the chair and once again looked out at his alter ego across the street. "I'd save every last cat for her if it would make a difference."

"Yeah, well, you better fucking make it work. You've only got another two days. You better get on with it."

I stood to leave, not really sure where I was going, since I had to connect with Louis, but I had to get out of there.

"What will you do now?" Garth asked.

"I don't really know. I guess I'm in for more of these Christmas miracles," I said, doing my best Santa impression. "I'm pretty sure I'm stuck with that fucking punk-ass English guy for a while. I gotta give him props, he's pretty damn good at this intervention shit. Kinda reminds me of what I did as a firefighter, you know, saving lives? But he's got some real mojo. You see the way he just knocked that guy out? Speaking of which—"

In a blur, Louis returned and whisked the three of us outta there as some badass federal agents came in and locked Blake in handcuffs. We watched from the gargoyle's ledge across the street as they went through the place, collecting evidence and shit. It took all night, but they left with everything of value and a very distraught-looking Blake.

"Good fucking riddance," I said as they shut the door.

"Yeah, out with the rubbish, in with the new. Mr. Stone, here is your deed to the penthouse and all of the codes and information you'll need to take over your new residence. Let's not find the joint crawling with scum and riffraff again. Anyone looking for our old friend Blake will experience a strange compulsion, keeping them away. Don't ask how it works."

Stone took the file from Louis and nodded. "Thank you, I guess? I promise, I'll—"

"You do that."

The sun began to rise in the distance, casting a glow over the building. We all watched as Kimberly woke from sleep and moved about her apartment, petting all of the cats as she fed them in the kitchen.

"Time to let him get to work," Louis said, gesturing toward Stone. "Good luck, mate." And then he and I were sucked into the blackness.

Chapter Ten

I had a plan. I returned to the alley where I'd fed the cat. He wasn't going to like this, but I was out of options. I had just over a day to make Kimberly see she belonged with me. I hoped my plan would work.

"I have a proposition for you," I called out, feeling like an idiot.

You again? You bring more fish? That shit was hella good.

"I'll give you all the fish you want, but I need a favor."

The mangy cat came strolling out from behind a Dumpster and sat in front of me, his tail swishing behind him. He looked as though he could be a real handsome creature with his fluffy orange and white coat. His green eyes hinted at an intelligence more sophisticated than humans would usually attribute to a cat.

Why do I get the feeling I'm not going to like this?

"You're not. At least not in the beginning. Look, do you believe in love?"

I'm a fucking cat. What do you think?

"I need to win over the woman of my destiny. She loves cats. Saving cats, to be exact. If I can show her that I support her dreams, maybe she'll—"

The cat held up a paw. *Hold up. This would involve me going to the pound, wouldn't it?*

"Just temporarily," I said, pleading with the cat now. "Come on. It'll just be over night. You allow yourself to get picked up, then I come in the next day and adopt you. You'll live in luxury on top of the city with all the fish you can eat."

More tail swishing. *How can I trust you?*

"You have my word." I knelt down and held out a hand. The cat stared at me for a moment, and before I could react, he swiped at my hand with a claw, drawing blood on my finger.

"Ow! Son of a—"

The cat licked at his paw and flinched. *You aren't human.*

"I'm something. I can't really say."

The cat nodded. *Good. You can't trust humans for shit. I'll go along with this, but if you don't come adopt me, I'll haunt your ass for eternity.*

"Fair enough."

Chapter Eleven

I pushed open the door and felt a rush of fear when I saw her standing behind the counter. With her hair pulled back, she looked so different than when I'd spent the night with her. Gone was the softness and humor I'd experienced. The look she gave me told me she was not pleased to see me.

She started to speak, but I cut her off. "I'm here to adopt a cat."

Her mouth snapped close in surprise. "A cat."

"Yes. I've just moved into a new apartment and I feel as though a furry friend would make it much more homey." I tried my winning smile on her. It did nothing.

"Really. Well. There are forms. And you'll need to have references. You can't just walk in here and get a cat, you know."

She tucked an imaginary stray hair behind her ear and her eyes darted around the office to see if anyone else noticed our back and forth.

"I'd still like to see who you might have available for adoption. The sign says visiting hours are open. May I visit?"

I was pushing my luck here, I just knew it.

"I told you this couldn't happen," she said.

"And I'm afraid I just can't walk away from you," I replied.

Her face flushed and she took in a shaky breath.

"You can't just walk in here and… There are rules!"

I heard snickers behind me, and Kimberly looked around me to give someone the stink eye.

"Please?" I asked, resting my elbows on the counter. "May I please see your cats? I promise I'll be gentle."

She paused for a moment. Seeing no way out of this visit, she rolled her eyes and growled loudly, eliciting more snickers from her office mates.

"Oh, fine. You can see the cats. Then will you leave?"

It was too bad for her I'd been programmed to be stubborn at some point. Maybe that whole being a rock for eons explained it.

"Maybe," I said with a wink and a smile.

She growled again, grabbed a ring of keys and stormed out from behind the counter and up the stairs. I glanced behind me, and an older woman in a similar uniform shooed me after her.

"Don't let her get away," she stage-whispered.

I didn't intend to.

"Here's who we have, but they're all older and quite a few have medical needs, so you probably won't be interested. We don't have any kittens, if that's what you're looking for."

I perused the cages, and the entire selection looked pretty pissed off to be locked up.

Great, some other schmuck here to poke at me through the bars and then leave. Just what I always wanted, to be locked up in a 3x3 for the rest of my life. Awesome.

So many thoughts in my head all at once. I was listening for a specific one when I realized she was still talking to me.

"Did you say something?" I asked her.

"Yeah, weren't you listening? God. Garth, why are you really here? I know it's not to adopt a cat."

You better have come to break me out.

Ah. Just the one I was listening for. My alley friend was at the very end. I walked to his cage to find him sitting and staring at me, his tail swishing.

"He's not available," Kimberly said.

Both the cat and I turned to look at her.

She did not just say that. You better get me out of here, asshole. You gave me your word!

"He just came in. We need to have him see the vet. If he passes his vet check, he'll be available tomorrow."

"Then I'll wait," I said hurriedly. There was no way I was leaving my alley friend in here a moment longer than necessary, and I shot him a look to express that. He still did not look pleased.

"He's probably going to need special care. I think he's older and he's got a major flea infestation."

"I don't care. He's the cat for me. What do I need to do?"

She crossed her arms over her chest. "You're serious, aren't you?" Her voice was softer now, almost like it had been our first night together.

"He's important. I need him."

You're so extra. Just tell her the truth. You're scared of me because I'll haunt you—

"Well, you'll need to fill out paperwork. He's not chipped, so he's obviously a stray. Our vet will want to neuter him too. We have a policy."

The fuck she just say?

I shot him a look of apology and he started pacing.

"Are you sure that's necessary? He'll be indoors only and—"

"No snip, no trip. He doesn't leave here with his balls."

I'll get you for this.

"I'll make it up to you," I said to the cat, although I had no idea how that was even possible. I'd only had man parts for a short time and I was already quite attached to them.

Kimberly watched me interact with the cat curiously. Alley Cat did me a favor and brushed against the bars of the cage, as if he wanted me to pet him. I reached out a hand and he nuzzled it with his jaw.

"He's been totally standoffish with everyone since he got here yesterday. Guess he likes you."

"Feeling's mutual," I murmured.

I'll scratch your eyes out while you sleep if you don't get me out of here. I'll escape and I'll find you.

"Let's, uh, see about that paperwork."

I followed Kimberly back down to the counter, where she handed me a clipboard with papers on it. The print on it scrambled around in front of my eyes until I figured out what it said. My first time reading. *Hurray.* Now let's see if I could actually write.

"You can sit over there and fill this out." Kimberly pointed to a bench near a window, apparently needing a little space from me.

I sat there and looked around for a few minutes, worrying unnecessarily how I was going to do this. Once my hand got with the program, the words just flowed from the pen. I snickered as I realized what I was writing.

Employer: Sheffield Security

Position: Security Specialist, Surveillance

House or Apartment: Penthouse

Years at address:

How was I supposed to answer that? *Yeah, I've been watching the penthouse for many, many years. Creep.*

If renting, does landlord allow pets?

Apparently. I own the penthouse.

A man sat next to me with a clipboard, and I jumped when I realized it was Louis.

"Really need to get a cat for my gran," he mumbled. His eyes darted to the side to look around and see if we were being watched. "Don't worry so much, mate," he whispered. "This is going to work out. Your feline friend will get sprung tomorrow, just without his balls." He put the back of his hand to his mouth to stifle a laugh.

"Yeah, but Louis, how am I supposed to—"

"Beats me, but you've got until tomorrow. Better make it good." He waved a hand and the rest of my form was filled out.

"How did you do that?"

Louis shrugged. "Don't really know. Whatever I need done to make my interventions work just seems to happen. Lucky, I suppose. Go on, then. It's almost closing time. Here," he said, slipping me a newspaper clipping. "This is where you should take her."

I unfolded the clipping and thought Louis just might be a genius.

I stood and brought my clipboard back up to Kimberly at the counter. She stared at me as though she wanted to say something, but she was at war with her desires. I knew this to be true. She had to have felt the chemistry between us. The magic. Whatever you wanted to call it, we had it. Whether it was because of Tommy and Louis and this intervention, I had no idea. All I knew was that I was made for her, and I'd never survive if she didn't accept me. What that meant for my future remained to be seen. I hoped I didn't have to find out.

Kimberly reached for my clipboard and I covered her hand with my much larger one.

"Let me take you out tonight."

She pulled her hand back like I'd burned her. "Please don't do this, Garth. You know I can't."

Her eyes began to fill with tears behind her thick glasses. I reached over and ran my thumb across her cheek.

"I know you're afraid. I promise, I just want to show you something. No funny business."

Her look of frustration was probably meant to chase me off, but she was so adorable when she frowned at me like that, I couldn't help the grin that spread across my face.

"I'll pick you up tonight."

She nodded slowly, and my grin must have been contagious because she gave up fighting her urge to smile.

Chapter Twelve

When I arrived at her apartment, I knocked on the door and waited impatiently. I knew exactly where I was and who I was going to see this time. I couldn't wait. I just hoped what I had planned would be enough.

Kimberly opened the door with a frown on her face.

"I don't think this is a good idea. Derek has been a little sick and I don't want the other cats to—"

Get her out of here pleaaaase! If she sticks that thing up my butt one more time I'm going to bite her.

Derek wandered over right then and brushed against my legs. I bent down to pick him up and Kimberly started to warn me.

"Don't, he doesn't like—"

The cat rubbed his head all over my jaw and purred loudly. At least I'd won over her cat, if not her heart.

"He's never done that before," she said, confused.

Two more cats approached, I think they were Elliot and Hank, and they meowed loudly.

You mess with her and we kill you.

Plain and simple.

You don't want to see what we've got cooking.

Now the cats were thinking wrestling insults. *Great.*

I set Derek down on the ground and he hurried back toward the cat tree she had in the corner, where three other cats were perched watching her. I forgot just how many she had, but they all seemed to be watching my moves closely.

"Fine. We'll go, but I don't want to be gone long." She muttered as she went toward the kitchen and I followed, giving her plenty of space. She hadn't dressed up much, not really. She wore a pair of worn jeans, boots, and a sweatshirt that said, "I Love Cats… You, not so much."

Message sent and received.

She began opening cans and the cats came running into the kitchen, each of them brushing against my leg as they passed.

Don't mess this up.

I smiled, glad to sort of have their approval.

"What are you laughing at?" Kimberly's frown was fierce, her lips turned down at the corners. Her dark eyes were round behind her thick glasses.

"Nothing, just seems like you have a well-oiled machine in here."

She washed her hands, keeping any further thoughts to herself. I watched her as she pulled on a thick wool coat and pulled her hair out from underneath it. "I'm ready," she said, sounding completely unready.

I held out my arm for her and she reluctantly took it.

We'll be waiting.

"Don't worry. I'll have her home soon."

It was a few blocks' walk to Kit Tea, a tea shop and cat adoption center on Gough. As soon as we approached the windows, Kimberly paused.

"What better place to take you on a date?"

She looked at me, puzzled. "You drink tea?"

I smiled at her and loved the way she stood next to me, sort of pressed against my side. We really did fit well together. Before I got lost in the moment and started picturing her pregnant with my child... "Let's get you inside. You must be cold."

I'd called ahead to make reservations and booked the cat lounge, so we could have it to ourselves. The seating wasn't quite made for a large being such as myself, so I took a seat on the floor and was immediately covered in cats.

You smell like cats

You smell like hope. Take me home?

Don't even think of adopting her. She shits outside the box.

Do not.

Do too.

"How did you find this place?"

Kimberly hadn't spoken until now, and the wonder in her voice startled me.

"A friend. My employer, actually." I had to keep the chuckle out of my voice. "I guess they just opened about a week or so ago."

"It's amazing! I've read about these cafes in Japan. I'd love to open my own sanctuary for cats, for the ones no one wants. I want to offer a place for them to go and live out their days peacefully." She laughed, but it was laced with sadness. "My husband always thought it was a pipe dream. He wanted me to be happy, sure, but he didn't have vision when it came to that stuff. Plus, he hated cats."

"I think you should do what makes you happy."

I could live a thousand years and never experience the beauty of the smile she gave me right then ever again. She was radiant. And then it was gone.

"You never said what sort of work you do," she said, obviously uncomfortable talking about herself.

Once again, the words needed at the moment came pouring out. "Security. I work for a private security company."

She frowned. "That sounds made up."

"Not in the least. I just worked a job yesterday that ended in the release of some victims of human trafficking."

I didn't mean to sound boastful, but I wanted her to see I was someone she could trust, that she could lean on.

"Now it sounds dangerous."

I shrugged. "I'm careful. I have backup when necessary."

I noticed she was scratching at her neck. She took off her coat and laid it over a chair, but her neck was all red over the top of her sweatshirt.

"Are you okay?" I asked.

"Huh? Oh. That coat just makes me itch, that's all."

I shook my head. "Then why wear it? That seems uncomfortable."

She was petting the out-of-the-box shitter and the serene look she had faded quickly. "It was a gift from my husband."

As if that explained why she'd walk around with a rash.

"I didn't mean for you to get rid of it, but why not wear something—"

"Because, alright? I told you, he's my husband. He may be dead, but—"

"But what? Are you just waiting to join him?"

I knew it was a shitty thing to say before the cats' thoughts all echoed my realization.

Low blow.

Someone ain't getting laid tonight.

Dumbass.

"I'm sorry, I—"

"You know what your problem is, Garth? You come into my life and you're supposed to be just a one-night thing. All of a sudden, you think you know what's best for me? I've been on my own for years now. I think I know how to take care of myself, thank you."

She stood to leave but the cats, God bless them, blocked her path. She reached for her coat and a cat leaped onto it, meowing at her.

"I just want you to be happy, Kimberly. That's all. I want you to live for *you*, not for a dead guy who didn't appreciate what a treasure he had."

The pain in her eyes when she looked at me told me I'd hit my mark. I didn't want to hurt her, not at all. But I wanted her to realize that she was hurting, and that I could ease her pain. I wanted to give her the life and happiness she deserved, and not just because Tommy had instructed me to. I'd watched her cry for so long over memories of him. I wanted more for her.

"Please," she whispered. "I don't want to hurt you. I just can't do this."

"Or won't."

I didn't know what else to do. I stood, ignoring the thoughts of protest from my furry friends. "Listen, Kimberly. I don't claim to have all of the answers, but I do know the two of us were thrown together for a reason. I want to honor your feelings, but I also want you to accept that there's more for you out there than promises made to a dead husband. He wouldn't want you to grieve for the rest of your life. I know, because even if you don't choose me, *I* still wouldn't want you to grieve for the rest of your life."

She swallowed hard and wiped at her face. "This was a mistake," she said, snatching her coat from underneath the cat and hurrying out the door.

Harsh.

I'm sorry, man.

You're better off without her.

"Women, good for nothing but heartache."

I turned to find the last thought had come out of Louis's mouth.

"I wouldn't know," I said. "This is my first heartache."

The cats all started backing away from the two of us, hissing with their ears back.

Evil!

Danger.

Get him!

I had no time to react. Out-of-the-box shitter leaped at Louis and attached herself to his back.

"Bloody hell!" he shouted, and it all broke loose. Cats darted around the room, swiping at him as he flailed, trying to knock the cat off his back.

"Don't move!" I reached for her and she leaped into my arms, turned back towards him and spit, growling like something out of the horror movies I'd seen the guys watching in the apartment below Kimberly's.

"You stay back, you beasts!" Louis tried to look terrifying. I didn't have the heart to tell him that these cats could take him out easy.

"You'd better leave," I said to him as he backed toward the door, tripping over a cat and falling into the glass.

"Is something wrong?" The owner of the shop came in looking horrified. "What's going on?"

"My friend has a problem around cats. They just don't like him for some reason. I was trying to see if this Zen-like establishment would help, but obviously —"

"Get him out of here," she shouted, pointing her finger at Louis.

"Don't get your knickers in a twist over a few angry pussies." He gave her an evil wink and she shrieked.

"Get out before I call the police!"

I handed her the out-of-box shitter and smiled. "I'm terribly sorry for the disruption." I handed her several hundred-dollar bills. "I hope this covers it. Thanks for the tea!"

Louis and I hurried into the street before anything else could happen. He was still cursing. "I don't know what your lady friend sees in those hellish beasts, but if I never see another cat, I will be a happy man."

"Feeling's apparently mutual. Man, they really hate you. Why do you think that is?"

He shrugged. "Probably it's my animal magnetism. It's just too much for them. They can't take it. Either that or I was a dog in a previous life."

I barked out a laugh. "You know, you're alright. You act as though you hate the world, but you're alright in my book."

"Yeah, well, no accounting for taste." He looked down at a pocket watch. "Time's running out, mate. You have less than twenty-four hours to make this work, or else I have to return you to your ledge."

I knew what he said was true. "At least there, I'll still be able to watch over her. Not that I can do much, but I'll still be close."

"Sad lot that would be. Look, don't give up yet. You've still got to rescue your friend. You'll think of something."

Yeah. If nothing else, I could hopefully spring my alley cat friend and give him a better life. Somewhere.

I had one last chance.

Chapter Thirteen

It was Christmas Eve and the amount of traffic around the city was insane. I shook my head as I walked along the sidewalk on my way to the Animal Care and Control Center. These people were oblivious to the good lives they led.

I'd spent the day handing out money all over the city to homeless people freezing in the streets. My wallet just kept refilling itself every time I gave some to an unfortunate person. If I was going back to my ledge tonight, I wanted to spread as much happiness as possible. That way, maybe the rest of my existence, I would see some humanity, rather than the awful ways people treated each other. It was worth a shot.

I'd returned to the penthouse long enough to clean up and take a look around before saying goodbye. Who knew who would end up there next?

That was when it hit me.

Well, when I looked up and noticed the way the wood beams ran the width of the penthouse under the vaulted ceilings and along the tops of the walls. They were perfect for a cat, and there were tons of them all over the penthouse.

Between the windows and the beams, a cat would be in heaven up here. Too bad I—

I had my answer. If I couldn't have Kimberly, I could give her what she wanted most in this world.

Outside the shelter where she worked, I took one last moment to catch my breath and prayed she would accept my offer.

I pushed open the door, and the look on her face almost sent me running for my life.

"We close in fifteen minutes. You need to—"

I handed her an envelope. "I have a proposition for you."

"Garth, I told you to forget it."

I held up a hand. "Just hear me out. I heard what you said and I want to make it happen for you."

She frowned. "What are you talking about?"

"The sanctuary. You want a place for cats to go? I have such a place. I'm being transferred," I said, my voice cracking. I wasn't sure I could get out my speech as I'd practiced it without breaking down, but this was it. I had to try.

"I'm leaving you the perfect place to open your sanctuary and enough money to keep it running for a lifetime. My attorney drew up all of the paperwork today," I lied. Louis definitely wasn't an attorney, but he'd been willing to come through for me once I explained my plan.

"The only catch is that you have to make sure you take that cat I wanted to adopt with you. He deserves a life of luxury. And fish. Lots of fish."

"Are you crazy or something? That's it, isn't it? Oh, Garth. You need help. Maybe there's someone we can call?"

I nodded toward the envelope. "You should have everything you need. If not, call the number on the letterhead. And Kimberly?"

She had opened the letter and was reading it with eyes bugging out of her head. She looked up at me in total confusion.

"Take care of yourself, too. The cats need you."

I nodded to her, turned around, and took the hardest steps of my life out the door—and out of her life forever.

I'd walked a block away when I heard footsteps pounding the pavement behind me.

"Will you stop? God dammit, you walk fast," she said between pants.

"Was there something missing in the documents? I thought everything was clear."

"Yeah, everything was clear. Clearly you're insane! Why would you do this, Garth? You hardly know me."

"I know enough to know you are the most amazing human being I've ever met and I want you to be happy. That's all I needed to know."

I turned and walked away from her, the pain in my chest growing with each step. My movements were becoming stiff and everything hurt, as if this body was beginning to reject me. I just needed to get back to my ledge and—

"Wait! I can't accept this! I can't do this on my own. I need—"

"Everything you need—"

"Is right here." She had her hands on her hips and a look that meant business on her face. "I need a partner, you know? I need someone I can trust to do this with me."

I looked back towards her work. "I'm sure there's someone you work with who loves cats as much as you." I couldn't take much more of this. "Kimberly, you've been clear from the start that you didn't want more than one night. I shouldn't have pushed it."

"You were right, though. I need you...to be my partner. In this business venture. Together. I can't promise you more than that right now."

Hope fluttered in my chest as she moved closer to me.

"I wouldn't want you to promise anything else," I said, hoping this was enough, that I'd be allowed to stay with her.

"It's just, I'm not ready to be anything more than business partners—"

"Then business partners it is."

She stood directly in front of me, that itchy coat making her neck red. I had to force myself to just breathe rather than take her in my arms.

"Um," she said, her eyes darting side to side as she laughed. "Should we shake on it or something?"

I reached down and grasped her hand, bringing it to my chest over my heart. "It would be my honor to be your partner."

Her cheeks flushed from more than the cold and she pressed against me. She squeezed my hand and pushed up on her toes to kiss my cheek.

"Thank you, Garth. You're making my dreams come true."

This was only the beginning, I thought to myself. Before it was all said and done, every last dream she ever had would come true. My life literally depended on it.

"So, I'm guessing you can postpone your move?"

"Hmmm? Oh, for work? Yeah. I have a flexible schedule. I'm basically on-call."

She licked her lips. "Well, what do you say we go get our first resident?"

Alley Cat. "Definitely. I think it's only fitting he be our first. And you better let me handle him," I said, placing my arm hesitantly around her shoulders. Thankfully, she relaxed against me as we walked.

"I am a trained professional, you know," she teased.

"Right. Of course. But he and I bonded. We've both been around for a while, watching this town."

Kimberly snorted. "Well, don't let me get in the way of your male bonding."

I gave her a squeeze as we reentered the shelter to the applause of her coworkers. She tried to wiggle away from me, embarrassed by the attention.

"Let me just go get the keys," she said. I'd always remember the glow of her cheeks as she blushed.

We walked up the stairs, sneaking glances and smiles at each other, and when she opened the door, his was the first thought I heard.

About fucking time, asshole. The drugs wore off and I'm ready to kick your ass...

Chapter Fourteen

Louis and I watched as Kimberly and Rock Boy went over plans for their cat sanctuary in the penthouse above the streets of San Francisco. She'd never looked lovelier than she did as her face lit up, talking about those fucking hairy beasts.

"All's well that ends well, then?"

"Yeah," I said, wiping at my eyes. A bug flew in, alright? Don't get any fucking ideas. "Good luck to that guy. All them cats would drive me fucking bonkers."

Thing is, Stone looked just as happy as she did. Sure, he was sporting a nasty scratch on his cheek, probably from that mangy-ass cat they'd brought home a few hours ago. Kimberly had gaped at the penthouse in shock, but almost immediately she'd started pointing and asking questions about the place. Stone just grinned like the cat that ate the damn canary. Good for him.

"I just hope he gives her babies."

"I'm sure once she gets over her fear, they'll be going at it like rabbits in no time."

"Really? Come on! She's still my fucking wife."

"Yeah, yeah. You know what I meant. Listen up, Father Fuckin' Christmas, we've time for one more intervention before this year's holiday is over. You up for it?"

I glanced across the way once more and watched as Kimberly cuddled that mangy-ass cat in her arms, and sighed. *Be happy, baby. Let him give you everything I couldn't.*

"Whatcha got for me, boss?"

It was always so damned disorienting when that fuckin' guy whisked us away into the black hole of nausea and we popped up someplace new.

"Can't we just do that walking-forever bit? I'm gonna hurl you keep flashing us in and out..."

We were standing across the street from a house that looked just like one in my old Jersey neighborhood.

"What the hell are we doing here?" I asked Pin Cushion.

Louis lit up a smoke and took an insanely long drag on the damn thing. I wanted to smack it outta his mouth for making me wait.

"It seems the widow in this house is about to set the curtains on fire with her cigarette, as she's trying to put together her son's tricycle for Christmas morning. It sure would be grand if an off-duty fireman happened to be walking by and knocked on her door to lend a helping hand."

Louis waved a hand in my direction, and I felt pressure and then it released. I looked down at myself and stumbled over my own feet.

"What the fuck did you do?"

Louis shrugged, his smirk infuriating as all get out. "Returned you to a bit of your former glory, only with a different face. Can't have Fat Tommy Santa Claus accosting the local widow." He wiggled his eyebrows at me and took another hit on his smoke.

I looked real hard through the window of the house and could see a blonde in a sleep shirt and hot pants, pacing around the living room in front of the Christmas tree with a cigarette in one hand and a cell phone in the other.

"It seems the place she ordered the tricycle from forgot to include the instructions. Are you handy?"

The little shit was getting a kick out of this whole situation. I looked down again to see myself in a fire uniform. My heart pounded. This couldn't be right.

"Yes, you do deserve a second chance tonight, mate. Your sacrifice for Kimberly gave you a shot at a new life. Congratulations. Now get in there and show that widow just how handy you can be with your tool. And put that fire out."

Sure enough, she'd set her cigarette down in an ashtray too close to the curtains and a small flame erupted. It made its way slowly up the drape and also spread along the bottom.

"Get on it, then," Louis said, giving me a shove.

I turned to face him and found a genuine smile in the place usually occupied by a sneer.

"You're alright, Pin Cushion."

"Whatever," he said, kicking at a stone on the ground. He gestured with his chin. "You better get to work."

A squeal from inside the house let me know the woman had discovered her mistake. I looked to Louis once more to thank him, and he'd vanished. Only one thing left to do, then.

I took the steps two at a time and knocked on the door.

The blonde opened it with the phone pressed to her ear.

"Oh! How did you get here so soon? I hadn't even put in my address yet?"

I smiled, trying not to stare at her perfect tits. "Just happened to be walking by," I said, pushing the door open and stepping inside. "Where's your extinguisher?"

"In the pantry," she answered, jogging past me toward the kitchen.

I stopped in my tracks when I realized this was my old neighborhood. My good friend from St. Luke's lived here, in this house. We went to the academy together. Could it be this was his—

"Here! Can you put it out? My son!"

I hurriedly sprayed the extinguisher and the flames died instantly. I was grateful she had a working unit. So many of the houses I'd been in through the years only had ancient and broken ones.

The smoke alarm hadn't even been triggered, it all happened so fast.

"Oh my gawd, thank you," she said, throwing her arms around me. "I can't believe I almost—"

"It happens, ma'am. I was just on my way home from work and saw the flames in the window. Probably you should find a different spot for your ashtray."

I turned to head for the door, but she stepped in front of me.

"I can't thank you enough. I don't know how I would have explained to the son of a fireman that his mommy set the house on fire."

Big tears pooled in the corners of her eyes. What could I do but hug the grieving widow?

"There, there," I said, winging this whole sympathy bit. I'd never been that great at it. "Coulda happened to anyone."

She wiped at her eyes and pulled back a little. "I'm so sorry," she said with a laugh. "Thank you. Can I offer you a drink? Something? Anything for being in the right place at the right time?"

She looked me up and down in a completely non-innocent way. A drink wouldn't hurt nothing, now would it? I looked around her living room and smiled at the bike in pieces.

"Someone's gonna have a nice Christmas morning."

She groaned. "Not likely. I can't get the thing put together. They sent the wrong instructions or something. You need to be a fucking nuclear physicist to build this damn thing."

"Well," I said, taking a seat on her couch. "My degree is in fire science, but I think I can manage. You can get me that drink you offered while I get to work."

She placed a hand on her chest and pursed her lips. "You are a godsend. I'll be right back…what did you say your name was?"

"Fa— Uh, Frank. Frank Christian."

Her smile promised more than a drink for a thank you.

"I'll just call you my Christmas Miracle."

That's me, I thought. Father Fuckin' Christmas.

The End.

Stay Tuned for more Rock 'n' Romance in the Afterlife with Louis and Maggie!

Author's Note

Christmas is not my favorite time of the year. It's true. Those who know me are fully aware of my preference for Halloween and all the things that go bump in the night. But I am a sucker for tales of miracles and true love, so this is my version of a Christmas story and writing it brought me a lot of joy. I wish for everyone who struggles with the holidays to find something joyful in this tale as well. Thank you for joining me on this journey.

Acknowledgements

Special thanks to my goddesses Miranda Bly and DeAnne Taylor for participating in the live write that became Father F'in' Christmas. Your loyalty, friendship and whacked out imagination brought this story to life and that's awesome. Love you both!

To Kelli, it was awesome being back in the saddle with you. Thank you for sharing your wisdom and wit. You make my world a better place.

To Tonya Ridener for coming to my visual aide. I always enjoy collaborating with you, even when our brains hurt. Many thanks.

To Regan Kubecek, thank you for another fantastic cover illustration. I love how you see what's in my brain!

To Yosbe, you took care of business super quick and got things rolling. Thank you for being there for me!

To Agnieszka for always asking the tough questions, being my Polish Ambassador, and honestly, my Jiminy Cricket.

As always, to my partners in crime Ellay Branton and Kimberlie L. Faye, you both rock my world and our daily, sometimes hourly, chats keep me sane in the face of certain breakdown. I love you to pieces!

Thank you to my husband and children for putting up with this weird authory gig. I love you.

Connect With R.L. Merrill

I would love to connect with you! Here's where you can find me lurking: Facebook at:
www.facebook.com/rowritesrocknromance
Email at rlmerrillauthor@gmail.com
Twitter @rlmerrillauthor
And my groovy website: www.rlmerrillauthor.com where you can find my newsletter-y thingie and stay up-to-date with the latest from my world of Rock 'n' Romance! You can even pick up passwords to unlock short stories set in the Teacher, Haunted and The Rock Season worlds.

Reviews

Reviews are incredibly important to authors. If you enjoyed Father F'in' Christmas, please leave your review for others at Amazon, GoodReads, or whichever rooftop you'd like to shout it from!

See where it all started in this excerpt from Minded...

"You won't be alone in your task. You will be escorted by an entity who has had years of experience. Your escort will assuredly assist you in all affairs. He is quite skilled. He is waiting for you outside those doors. You will carry this with you," she said, leaning forward to hand Maggie the pocket watch.

Maggie turned it over in her hands, lovingly caressing the fleur-de-lis embossed on the top.

"The pocket watch is your talisman. It is not to tell time, but to remind you that you have a limited amount of time to complete your task. It will keep you grounded as you step back into a life you are no longer a part of. Time will not move as you are accustomed to. Never neglect your task: Mind your kin. Help them resurrect their harmony. When it's done, you will have a choice to make. Follow the path, or remain here."

Maggie jerked her head to look towards the blackness, only this time there was a set of double doors with an illuminated exit sign above. She turned back to ask Grandma what was happening. She was now alone in the circle.

Grandma had vanished, as had the invisible bonds that had held Maggie in place.

She stood shakily from her chair and sucked in a breath, smoothing down her dress. She wobbled on her three-inch heels as she moved towards the doors.

"At least I won't be alone in this," she muttered to herself. Her shoes clacked loudly on the gym floor. She clenched and unclenched her fists as she walked hesitantly towards the door. The metal handles were cold under her hands. She pushed gently, not surprised that nothing happened. Her gym doors in high school were like that. You had to practically body slam the damn handle to get them open, which was often disastrous for the person on the other side waiting to get in.

The next time she pushed, she threw her meager weight into it. The door flew open and she stumbled out into the hall, stepping out of her heel.

"Not the most practical shoes in the world." The annoyed voice sounded from off to the left of the doorway.

Silhouetted by a single light shining in the hallway, leaning against a row of lockers, stood Louis.

Maggie's mouth went dry as she watched him slowly raise his hands to light a cigarette using a classic Zippo lighter. He cupped the flame in his hands then took a long drag, the red-hot tip of the cigarette flaring brightly in the shadows.

"Before we take things further, you should know a few important rules. You may not leave my presence or you will end up right back here. Argue with my instructions or put one patent-leather-covered toe out of line and I will send your arse right back here. When your time is up, no matter the outcome—"

"I know, I know. My ass will be sent right back here. Got it. Do you hate everyone, or am I just special?"

"Party Girl, I don't give a damn about you, or anyone else for that matter. I have a job to do, whether I like it or not, and I do what I'm told. End of story."

"But why are you here? If you—"

"Listen. I'm not here for you. None of this is about *you*. All you need to know is that I always get the job done and my charges get sent on. That's it. So don't try to get to know me, or ask me my story. It's none of your bloody business."

His voice dripped sarcasm and disgust in a way Maggie had never experienced before. Instead of being hurt, she was determined to find out just what the hell his problem was. He had no idea who he was dealing with. She'd dealt with dudes way tougher than him.

Always up for a challenge, Maggie was exhilarated by the idea of breaking down his punk-rock attitude and discovering what made him tick. She had to have something else to focus on rather than the gravity of her situation.

She knew she was dead, so they could take their D.D.S. and shove it. What she struggled with the most was the fact that she'd let her boys down. She never should have let things get so out of hand. The last night of her mortal life, she'd attended the band's record release party. Their third studio album was hot off the presses and though it didn't show as much growth as she'd hoped, she knew there were at least a few hits the rock charts were going to go crazy over.

Maggie had taken a short trip home on the sly to see her mama and arrived back a day before the party. That was in December of 2011. She had been confident everything would go smoothly. She knew her colleague and good friend Sherry Jordan had everything under control. Thomas threw a fit when she returned, but she'd expected that.

What she *hadn't* expected was that she'd arrive at the party to find her boys—her precious brother, cousins, and friends—in such awful states of intoxication. Mage had been so high on cocaine he was having paranoid hallucinations. He kept telling her she had to make it stop, begged her to go home and not be at the club. It took all of her managing ability to get him onstage that night. Star was so shitfaced he fell over a chair and cut his eyebrow so deep she thought they'd have to take him to the ER before they could even play. Thankfully someone had butterfly bandages or the show would have been delayed by several hours. Jade and Marcus were practically getting laid in a back booth. There were several girls crawling all over them, blowing them under the table and flashing their tits in the boys' faces.

Maggie had little tolerance for women who had no respect for themselves like that. But the kicker had been the shouting match she'd gotten into with Devon.

"I don't give a fuck, Richard! You screwed up the mix on the last three songs! I should have been there to approve it, goddamn it!" Devon rarely got confrontational, but that night he'd had more than a few hard drinks and even did some cocaine with Mage before getting into a huge brawl with Richard, their sound mixer.

When Maggie told him to calm down, he pulled away from her and screamed, "Fuck off, Maggie! You should have fucking taken care of this! Fuck you!" He stormed off to the bathroom and that was the last time she'd seen him.

Shortly after, Thomas grabbed her by the arm, still pissed about her trip, and told her they had to go back to the office because there were some papers he needed to sign. He dragged her out to the parking lot as she protested the whole way.

"Thomas! I have to be here," she pleaded, yanking her arm from his grasp. "Can't you see this is all falling apart?"

Maggie continued to argue with him as they climbed in the car and he revved the engine. She forgot all about her seatbelt.

"If you cared so much for your precious Bones, you wouldn't have left. Now do your job as my *wife*."

Maggie begged him to go back, worried there would be more trouble, but trouble for her was just beginning. She recalled reaching for his arm, pleading with him as he swerved, and then...

"What they say about dying being painless when it happens in a split second? It's bullshit. I remember," she said as she and Louis walked down the dark hallway, his tall, lanky frame beside her. "I remember feeling weightless just before the glass shattered. I swear I think I felt all of the bones breaking in my face. Then I flew through the air, hit the pole, and landed sprawled on the grass. I remember it now like I'm watching it happen in a movie. It was just like that horrific scene from *Grindhouse*, remember? With Kurt Russell? Stunt Man Mike? No? You don't—"

"No. And everybody feels their death. You're not the only one to feel pain, Party Girl."

"Jesus! Asshole much? I do have a name, you know. Actually, I have several. My family called me Maggie, my husband called me—"

"Pain in the arse? No? How about loudmouthed narcissist? Wake up, Party Girl. You're not unique. Everybody dies. Everybody feels pain. The only reason you're important right now is because you need to fix what you let unravel."

Maggie was unaffected by his name-calling. She'd had enough experience with people to understand projection, deflection…all those tions. She flicked her curls back over her shoulder and stuck her chin out.

"So what's the plan then, Sir Snottypants? Where are you from, anyway? You sound British, but there's—"

"Like I said before," he interrupted with a singsong voice. "None of your bloody business. We go where we're meant."

Unsatisfied with his answer, she grabbed his arm and attempted to pull him to a stop. She managed to slow him and barely avoided breaking a heel.

"Fine. No more personal questions. For now. How do we proceed when we get to where we're going? Will they be able to see me? Will I interact with them? How does this work?"

"Bloody hell, you ask a lot of questions. Look, just follow my lead. No one will see us or what we do unless it is necessary, and then it will just happen. You are not in charge anymore, you're no manager. You may have to use those skills, however. It sounds as though we are headed into a right catastrophe that's been brewing, and before you open that pretty mouth one more time, I'll not be answering any more questions. Are we clear?"

"Crystal," she said.

Moments later, the air around them grew heavy with a familiar scent. The hallway darkened until Maggie felt completely enclosed in blackness.

She followed the sounds of Louis's footsteps next to hers and prayed she didn't step wrong and sprain an ankle.

Minded: A Haunted Story
Available on Amazon
https://goo.gl/6Wu2WB

And next up, Maggie and Louis complete their first task together in Blossomed: A Minded Story

Here's an excerpt:

The sound of his voice awakened her from her watery rebirth. She could hear it soar tenderly across the surface. When it stopped, she finally opened her eyes.

The saltwater was dark around her and stung her eyes. She blinked hard and then swam toward the faint light above. It felt eerily like her death, but she somehow knew things were different this time. She broke through the water and breathed for the first time in her new body. She saw the figure of a man and his dog walking away from the coast and her eyes followed them as they got into a car and drove away.

The woman was on autopilot. Her body seemed to know to swim to the shore, where she found a sandy area hidden by some bushes. She took a few moments to calm her breathing, shivering from the chilly air against her cold, wet skin. Instead of panicking, which she was pretty sure she would have done in her previous life, she laughed. And laughed. And laughed until her voice went hoarse.

She held out her arms and examined them. Everything looked different. She was meatier, her skin paler. The wet strands of hair that clung to her skin were shades of brown that seemed foreign to her. Her legs were longer and fuller. Of course, the body she remembered had been riddled with cancer. Being ill for months before finally succumbing to the disease had left her body wasted. *This* body was hearty, full of energy.

"If you keep on laughing, the whole world will know a naked, wet, formerly dead woman has just washed up out of the Bay. Get yourself together, woman."

The man's heavily accented voice startled her. She crawled farther into the bushes.

"Oh, for the love of the Old Chap! Dude, you might have a little more tact. Makes the job easier, or hadn't you noticed?" The woman's voice sounded playful, not angry.

The woman peeked out from behind the shrubs and blinked. Standing before her was a guy with a tall Mohawk, dressed like some punk rocker, and a beautiful woman with long locks of curly blonde hair, wearing a black party dress. They were complete opposites. His brooding stare intimidated, her flirtatious smile invited.

"I brought you some clothes," the woman said, approaching her with a small duffle. "There's also a new ID, money, credit cards, and keys to a car parked just over there in the lot," she said, gesturing with her thumb over her shoulder.

"I think I finally have Grandma convinced they can't just pop you guys in here with nothing and expect you to not freak out." The blonde winked and crossed her arms over her chest, accentuating her curvy figure.

"Go on and get dressed, then. We have things to explain to you." The man turned away and the woman made a face behind his back.

Who were these people?

"You ever hear the expression 'you catch more flies with sugar?'"

"No. It must be another one of your backwoods Louisiana phrases a proper person wouldn't be caught dead using."

She listened to the man and woman bantering back and forth, her teasing, him sounding annoyed. Once she finished dressing in black stretchy pants, tall black boots, and a long white tunic, she stepped out from behind the bushes.

"But I *am* dead, silly! And I don't care what you say; you have your own quirky British uppity sayings that are just as bad. Come on, Louis. Nobody says 'cock up' with a straight face."

The man, Louis, started with a comeback, and then his lips split into a reluctant smile. "Bloody hell, you do go on. It has nothing to do with... Never mind."

The woman smiled victoriously, then noticed her.

"Wow! You are stunning." The woman circled her and whistled low. "I'm Maggie, by the way." She stuck out her hand and flicked her head in the man's direction. "Don't mind Louis. He's so much fun to mess with. Now. You probably didn't get the whole deal from Grandma, but you were sent back for a reason. You have a task to complete. We all have to do one before we can move on, but in your case… You gotta help this dude. His name is Justin and he's a mess—"

"Margaret," Louis said in a singsong voice. "You're supposed to let her figure it out, darling. Wouldn't want to drop a clanger."

Maggie laughed at him, bending at the waist. "That is precious. You are so adorable when you try to insult me using your antiquated sayings. Come on, Good Charlotte! Let's get you prepped. The year is two thousand fourteen and you're in—"

"Two thousand fourteen? Are you serious?" So much time had passed! The last date she remembered was…

"It's been over thirty years, love. You passed just after I did. The world has changed a lot. People are still imbeciles, though. Bunch of bloody assholes, if you ask me."

"And we didn't. There are still plenty of good people." Maggie frowned at Louis and put her arm around the woman. Charlotte. She liked it. "Look. You will know what to do when the time is right. All the information you need to function in this time is up there in your fancy new brain. For now, let's get you to your car. Are you familiar with this area? You're in San Leandro, California."

Charlotte had to think. She'd driven some around the Bay Area. She'd grown up in Newark, which wasn't too far away. She remembered the Nimitz Freeway ran north to south, so if she could find that…

"Here we are," Maggie said as they approached a large vehicle. It was some sort of Honda, she recognized the symbol on the front, but she'd never seen anything like this.

"It's a big box! What—"

"They certainly have made cars uglier. Damn Americans want everything bigger. Don't they get it? They're killing the bloody planet with these beastly—"

"Alright, Mister Doom and Gloom. Can it!" Maggie may have been telling him what to do, but she was all sass and no bite. He seemed to be irritated with everything *but* her. Charlotte was so entertained by them she almost forgot why she was here.

"Do you have any questions?" Maggie was asking her.

Charlotte had a million, but one stood out.

"So whenever I do what I'm supposed to do, is that it? They'll take me back? Because I—"

"We've no return instructions for you. I'm not certain what that means. It appears the Old Chap Upstairs decided... Bloody hell. You must have something very important to accomplish, or must have made a great sacrifice—"

Charlotte held up a hand for him to stop. She didn't want to think about sacrifice or anything involving her past. What was done was done. "Fine. I guess I'll figure it out. So, um, where do I go? What do I do?"

Louis stepped up next to Maggie and put a hand on her shoulder as she started to speak, effectively silencing her. She looked up at him with an adoring expression and nodded.

"That's as much as we can say." Maggie stepped away from Louis and approached Charlotte one last time. "Here," she said, handing her a pocket watch. "Keep this. If you need us—"

"Margaret—"

"Oh whatever, dude! I got this. Don't I always got this?" He rolled his eyes and looked toward the sky, mumbling under his breath as he walked away. Maggie followed him toward the darkness that was rapidly dropping from the sky.

"You'll be great," Maggie called back to her. "Just remember: listen with your heart. You've come through the veil for a very good reason." Louis tugged at her and she protested. Then he swatted her on her ass. Hard. She yelped and took off chasing him in her heels, yelling all kinds of colorful profanity at him.

Charlotte smiled and then shook her head. As if being born from the water of the Bay wasn't strange enough, her two greeters...

She stood there wondering what the gigantic plastic doohickey attached to the keychain was for, then she noticed the buttons. Somehow it all made sense. She clicked the key fob. Once the door was open, she set the duffle on the driver's seat so she could rifle through its contents. Inside she found a passport, a wallet with a California driver's license... *Oh, for the love of God.*

"Charlotte Bay. Is my name. Really." She laughed and placed the documents back in the bag. She looked down at her clothes and shrugged. Hopefully she wouldn't look as out of place as she felt.

She tossed the duffle into the backseat and slid into the driver's seat, praying silently she remembered how to operate a motor vehicle after her time spent in wherever she'd been. The car appeared to be an automatic, thank goodness, and started right up.

Now if she only knew which direction to head…

Blossomed is Available on Amazon

https://goo.gl/QQUkQu

Maggie and Louis will be back with more adventures from the afterlife soon!

www.ingramcontent.com/pod-product-compliance
Lightning Source LLC
Chambersburg PA
CBHW030543130626
46552CB00006B/2406